EMERALD TO
ICE

EMERALD TO ICE

MATT COLBORN

To my good friends Sue and Rory,
who helped all the way.

CONTENTS

Foreword by Liz Williams   9

PART I Falling   11

Interlude 1   67

PART II Primavera   75

Interlude 2   115

PART III Summer's End   121

Interlude 3   179

PART IV Ascent   189

Acknowledgements   233

Chronology   236

FOREWORD BY LIZ WILLIAMS

Science Fiction has traditionally relied upon a 'sense of wonder.' That's what initially drew me to the genre as a young reader: I still remember the feeling of excitement in being transported from a suburban house in 1970s Gloucester to another planet, another world, inhabited by strange beings who were far removed from the people whom I knew. Jack Vance, Ray Bradbury, Ursula Le Guin and Leigh Brackett, to name but a few, all formed early influences on my own work and on the way that I approached the world. That feeling of discovery has never gone away; it has remained with me as a genre reader throughout the intervening years and it's something that I strive to generate in my own fiction. I'm constantly seeking to stretch the envelope, both in the books that I read, and the books that I write.

When I first read *Emerald to Ice*, I found again that sense of wonder. The sense of isolation of this far future human colony, divided into cybernetically augmented humans and traditional settlers is palpable. This is a universe in which the planets themselves are characters in the story, as much as the sentient humans and their alien contacts; inimical, dangerous worlds, meticulously chronicled and environmentally researched by the author, on which survival beyond a few days is a struggle. Our protagonists—enthusiastic yet practical Cheyara and cool, posthuman Heron—face a battle against time and the elements, but also against the threat posed by a group of humans who, having become total machines, are now returning as a terrifying gestalt force, and from idealists in their own society.

Themes of safety versus risk, idealism versus pragmatism, compassion versus the question of how far we can interfere in other societies, are all explored in this novella with a sophisticated and sympathetic approach to ethical dilemmas.

Emerald to Ice contains that traditional sense of wonder whilst engaging with some very modern concerns. If it is to evolve, Science Fiction, of all genres, must not remain static and reactionary: part of its work in the world is to reflect contemporary concerns through the perspective of enquiry. We are, as SF writers, hired as thought experimenters for the culture, whilst not throwing those old elements of adventure and wonder out with the bath water. This novella fulfils this remit admirably.

I
FALLING

"Suppose we find that intelligent life that we're so excited about looking for...suppose we bump into it out there? How will we treat it? How will we behave?"

Brian May, Starmus I, 2011.

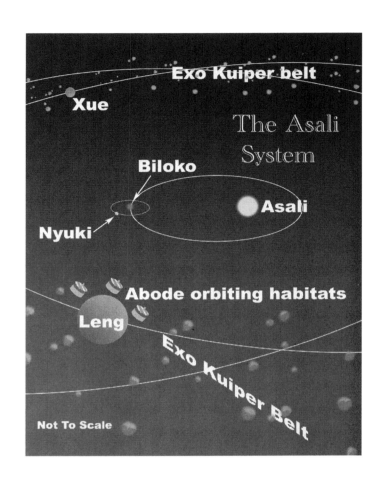

ASALI SYSTEM A.Y. 86

24TH AUGUST A.Y. 86

MISSION ELAPSED TIME: 0.1 Days before launch.
LOCATION: MSAFIRI IN SPACEDOCK.

That was when they let the Taiyangren engineers carry the objectors out. Three slender, lithe forms in pewter-tone skinsuits filed into the Msafiri's cargo hold, grabbing one rigid body after the other. One, two, three, four, five, six, seven.

Not one objector struggled: Sonja had told them to offer no resistance. Cheyara floated motionless beside Heron, watching the eviction. The wooden carving of the chlorelle was still in her hands. The pink-hatted Tranquillity Team seemed as paralysed as the Sentinel robots, spinning useless overhead.

Sonya was the last objector to be removed. She'd curled into the foetal position, forearms in cruciform over her chest, fists pallid and bunched. She bobbed in the microgravity between two Taiyangren, their prehensile feet propelling them through the airlock. When they'd gone, one of the pink-hats, Maya, moved to follow. The other pink-hat, Ramon, stopped her.

'We can't.'

'What do you mean?' Maya said. 'It's outrageous. They're community. We have to….'

'We can't,' Ramon said.

'Why not?'

'You know why.'

'You must leave.' said Heron.

'You knew about this, didn't you?' Maya said, to Heron.

'No.' said Heron.

'I don't believe you!'

'They'll be consequences,' Ramon said, before they left.

Then Cheyara and Heron were alone. Cheyara, clad in her flight suit and floating beside Heron, had bitten her tongue so hard that she tasted iron. Sonya's face was an afterimage, seared on her retina in luminous purple-orange-red. Heron was tugging her arm. She let em pull her along the passage to the flight deck. Heron's face remained expressionless in the bright red light.

Now they floated into the spherical flight deck. The walls were set to exterior view, real-time. Heron and she moved to the acceleration couches that were apparently floating in the middle of spacedock. Stars were visible in blackness beyond the grey-and-silver weblike nest of trusses in which the *Msafiri* was berthed. Beyond this the electromagnetic anti-radiation shield flared with a rainbow-coloured synthetic aurora.

Two pods were visible in mid-flight through the

shimmering, translucent veil. The Taiyangren pod led the mini-convoy. It was larger and pewter-coloured. Its hull was an elaborate biomechanical shell, etched with intricate patterns. There were no visible windows. The Tranquillity Team's pod trailed behind, crude and functional by comparison, a globular hull of off-white with manipulator arms.

Both pods caught the last light cast by the half-disk of their distant parent star, Asali, now setting behind the shrinking sepia-white limb of Leng. The pods moved slowly, almost imperceptibly across the dwarf planet's face. Their destination, Abode 1, hung in high orbit in the middle distance, half shrouded in shadow. Then Asali set and the near hemisphere of Leng was in darkness, a black-hole void in a universe of cold, glittering stars.

'You'd better stow that,' Heron said, 'then buckle up.'

She realised that she was still holding the carving. Heron gestured at the small locker beside the couch. She fumbled with the locker's lid, shutting the carving inside. Then she fastened her webbing as instructed.

The pods were moving faster now, following a lazy curve against stygian darkness. Bright LED lights illuminated the Abodan pod, but the Taiyangren pod glowed like a deep-sea creature. Heron had reached over and was fumbling with her webbing.

'Could you...?' Ey said. Cheyara looked down and saw that a strap was twisted.

'Sorry.' She undid herself, untwisting the webbing and rebuckling. Her hands, she saw, were shaking. Screwing her eyes shut, she took three deep breaths. Her heart throbbed in her ears, her thoughts racing like clouds in a hurricane.

Her personal display, relayed via neural lace, showed twenty seconds to launch.

Get a grip.

She imagined a ball of glowing light in the middle of her chest. Slowly, cardio-coherence returned and her thoughts slowed.

Ten second countdown. Sky-blue numbers flashing in her visual field.

…three, two, one.

The whole ship shook. An invisible force gently shoved her deeper into the couch. The *Msafiri* was firing its manoeuvring thrusters, piloting itself out of spacedock.

Minutes ticked by.

The silver-and-grey web of trusses was left behind as the ship moved into a pre-set orbital trajectory.

The main engines fired.

As the acceleration increased, she had the sensation of the flight deck tipping backwards until she lay on her back. They were now apparently hurtling upwards. This was an illusion, a conspiracy between her vestibular system and her brain. It was a reality that was local to Heron and she. But in another sense, the ship was not rising but falling. Falling as it began its slow, spiralling descent into Asali's gravity well.

Minutes fled past. They had little to do but watch the displays and the changing scene outside. It was all automated. They were not crew, they were cargo. Now Abode 1 was far behind them and the irradiated, frozen, enshadowed globe of Leng had begun to shrink.

There will be consequences, Ramon had said.

And it had all seemed so simple.

7TH MAY A.Y. 86

MISSION ELAPSED TIME: 109 Days before Launch. LOCATION: SURFACE OF DWARF PLANET LENG, ASALI KUIPER BELT.

Four months previously….

A notification pinged on Cheyara's helmet display. She blinked, opening the message window. The Matua had been spotted on the mountainside.

'Fuck!' !

.

She leaned on the bowed line that had been strung on poles down the slope.

'What's the matter?' Elias said from behind her, up the slope. Azleena was downhill, below her.

'Oh, nothing….'

Cheyara thrust with her foot, launching herself forward. She was too vigorous, and only the tether hooked to her waist prevented her from shooting over Alzeena's head. Settling on the icy slope, she steadied herself before unbuckling from the tether and trying again. This time her arc was more modest and she landed less than two metres behind the other woman. She grappled for the line but missed, toppling in treacle.

Whoops.

She tapped the ground with her right foot which arrested her sideways drift and allowed her to grab the line which undulated slowly in protest. Cheyara caught her breath. You really can't hurry in one-twelfth Earth-gravity, wearing crampons on a forty degree slope.

'You okay?' Azleena said, looking back, the light of Asali glinting off the top of her helmet. Cheyara made the 'okay' sign with her fingers. Then the comms channel closed and the only sounds were Cheyara's breathing and the whirring suit. Azleena turned away and took another two steps down the slope. Her movements were as careful and exact as a ballet dancer. Cheyara gritted her teeth.

Abodes 4 and 5 were above the horizon, bright stars in high geostationary orbit. Asali's discernible disk outshone them and was bright enough to illuminate the dwarf planet's frozen surface and dim the stars in the velvet sky. The smaller, dimmer reddish disk of Biloko swam some distance from its parent star. An ignorant observer might dismiss Biloko as inconsequential. This would be a mistake. There was a livestream coming from a planet in its orbit that Cheyara was desperate to see.

Cheyara took another couple of careful bounds forward and paused. Dammit, why was she so breathless? She checked her suit life support display, but everything was nominal. She was stressing herself unnecessarily.

'That's right, take your time,' Elias said.

Slow was fine, but she couldn't stay put. The mountain on which she stood was composed of water ice with a reddish brown-ochre tinted, tholine impregnated surface. Temperatures were so low on Leng that the ice was as solid as rock. The surface cold was seeping through the soles of her allegedly warmed boots and her feet were already almost numb. If she stayed in place her legs would freeze completely and they'd have to carry her down the slope. Then she'd miss even more of the livestream.

She was still gasping like a goldfish.

She screwed her eyes shut, telling herself that she had time, that the Matua would be slow and anyway it was no use if she had a fatal accident. The neural lace was scribbling bossy warning messages across her upper visual field. She slowed her breath deliberately, using *Kapalabhati* breathing. Her ankles were now aching with cold. Her feet were two insensible lumps.

'Now try again.' Elias said.

Cheyara began to move in slow bounds downhill. The light scree of brittle ice that littered the slope like icing sugar crunched beneath her feet. She slipped several times on the descent, each potential pratfall forcing her to pause and regain her balance whilst panting like a dog. Azleena was already at the bottom, waiting patiently for her companions.

Cheyara was sweating too much. The drops drifted around her face in the almost-but-not-quite-microgravity, only slowly ambling downwards. She always sweated too much in these suits, and they were tight around the shoulders. Damn the sweat and damn the cold!

She was descending the last foothill of a range of jagged mountains that formed a broad barrier cutting off the sepia-stained plain below. The plain was the site of a temporary base about half a klick from the base of the range. The base was composed of inflated domes and cargo containers with comms arrays and a park for three large 'Monster' rovers with pressurised cabins and enormous tyres. Beyond the base was a launch field where two small orbital shuttles perched on spindly legs.

Eventually she reached the bottom of the slope, almost slipping on her backside when she was less than a metre from the plain. She cursed her slow and clumsy movements which three months on Leng and quite a few mountain treks had done little to alleviate. Despite everything, she loved the mountains, although the extreme conditions too often negated the sublimity of the experience.

'Low gravity's a bastard.' Elias said, joining her at the bottom.

'Yup.'

All three of them trooped back to base.

Twenty minutes later, she removed her helmet in the airlock. The inner lock opened and they entered the base. They had a debriefing in the main dome. Cheyara kept glancing at the clock throughout. Eventually, they let her go. She made a beeline for her cabin, which smelt of burnt coffee. Her forearms were still numb from the cold so she had to massage them before she could squeeze the correct skinterface. Finally, stomach fluttering, she got the Supalite livestream running.

The first image materialised above Cheyara's cluttered bed showing a slope strewn with snow-covered rocks beneath a cloudy sky. The parent star Biloko had just risen behind clouds, lending a reddish-pink caste to the scene. She was lucky. The signal was strong today, with minimal electromagnetic interference from the volatile Biloko.

The drone was positioned at a height of about four metres. It was one of a myriad of similar drones that had been placed on Nyuki, machines that ranged in size from a *paramecium* to a small bird. Now, in semi-darkness and with negligible gravity, Cheyara felt almost as if she were floating like a balloon. She closed her eyes to enhance the effect, flipping into full immersion mode. Mimesis level was about six: audiovisual only, without haptics and olfactory input.

It was still snowing, but lightly.

A red-brown figure was picking its way amongst dark rocks. It had a shuffling gait and left blurred tracks in the snow. From above the Matua was difficult to make out against the jumble of grey-brown rocks and white snow. Once or twice she paused, almost disappearing against the rock field.

At one point the Matua slipped and fell, her palms slapping an ice-slicked boulder. Her hands clawed the slippery surface. For a moment Cheyara thought that she'd slide all the way, smashing her face on the rock. Then the Matua gained purchase, her four-digit spiderhands gripping the cold grey surface. Her chest rose and fell as steam huffed from spiracles on the face and chest. Bent over, her belly visibly bulged. Then she walked backwards with her hands, gradually reassuming an upright position. When she was fully erect she resumed her shuffling walk.

The drone ascended slightly, revealing more of the broad, desolate slope. The Matua looked like an ant crawling on a whitewashed wall, a gracile almost-hominoid lost in a white wilderness. But *hominoid* wasn't quite the right analogy, except perhaps from afar, with a squint. An eye blink and the humble seemed more like an ambulatory owl with gangly legs. Another blink and the occasional tic of the Matua's head seemed almost insectile.

The Matua's journey was propelled by blind instinct. Nothing short of crippling injury or death would stop the Matua reaching her destination: not semi-starvation, freezing cold, treacherously uneven terrain, crevasses, rockfalls or avalanches, or the large predators that would now be waking hungry. Cheyara recalled videos from the Earthian Archive, showing male salmon swimming upstream to their mating ground. The salmon mated, and died.

Here, the situation was different, yet broadly comparable. As with the salmon, biology and evolution had assigned the Matua a sacred purpose. Or maybe a grim fate.

The Matua lurched over a small, yellow-white some-thing that squatted on the ground. The ermine flitter flapped away from the advancing Matua at a crazy angle, swooping over the broken array of snow-covered boulders.

The Matua paused directly underneath the drone, which zoomed downwards. The down on top of her head looked patchy and for a moment Cheyara worried that the Matua might be diseased. Perhaps she had some mange-like illness. Then she remembered that the humble would have begun her springtime moult. These were the last five days of the Melt season. Temperatures had risen dramatically over the last ninety-five days and the Matua's body was fast adapting to the changing seasons.

The drone turned, tracking the Matua's zigzag descent. The pan revealed the lower slopes of the mountain, van-ishing into a thick mist. The snow in the bottom of some sheltered valleys had begun to thaw, expelling water vapour into the atmosphere. That trend would accelerate in the weeks to come.

Cheyara glanced at the time-stamp on the images, not-ing a twenty minute lag. Nyuki was about five light-hours distant, but the image would have been relayed to Abode 1 via Supalite almost instantaneously. The conventional EM signal relay from Abode 1 to Leng probably accounted for the delay.

A notification pinged into her visual field.

Elias.

Fuck! She'd forgotten.

She reluctantly flipped off the livestream.

*

Elias spoke in a monotone when he was in training mode, with less inflection than the base AIs. Cheyara, already physically exhausted, found herself zoning out. A portion of the transparent wall of the dome was visible over his shoulder and she had a view of the double stars, still above Leng's horizon. Biloko was like a glowing coal beside the magnesium-flare of Asali.

Then Elias called her to the bench and she was going over spacesuit checks, for the umpteenth time.

'Not like that.' Elias said, as she fumbled with an air hose.

She had to start again.

Next, an even worse torture session, AKA Field Medicine. Azleena led this one and actually it ended up more a laugh than a torture session. Today's skill: fitting a catheter.

'I'm not a nurse!' Cheyara said, beating the table with a rubber penis.

'You certainly aren't!' Azleena said.

Afterwards, Azleena wanted to gossip over coffee. There were rumours circulating, she said. Rumours that the Taiyangren had discovered something in the Samudra system. At the time, Cheyara hardly listened. The rumour seemed so trifling, one of many whispers, mostly false, that made their rounds on the Community Cloud. Much later, she wondered whether it would have made a difference if she'd paid attention.

*

Afterwards she grabbed an extra cup of coffee and returned to her room. The Matua was following the course of an immense cataract that roared down the snow-covered mountainside. The cataract carried large chunks of ice on lead-coloured, swirling waters. It thundered over rocks, kicking up fountains of spray. The cataract was at least a hundred metres wide and the racing, frothing waters threatened to overwhelm the bank on which the Matua trekked. She paused as a large, car-sized chunk of ice became momentarily trapped by a fortress of rocks in the middle of the course. The ice chunk turned slowly in the water, pivoting on the rocks. Then, given a fresh spin by the torrent, it sped on its way, heading for the valley below.

The drone had descended to hover almost parallel to the Matua. Despite the moulting patches, Cheyara saw that she still retained most of her thick, red-brown winter fur. She was certainly in need of insulation on this descent. Saturated, the Matua blinked slowly, wiping spray from her eyes before she continued her scramble over wet, icy rocks. She seemed unphased by the frothing waters about a metre below.

Cheyara closed her eyes, flipping the livestream into full immersion mode. The noise of the river was too loud and her neural lace, registering mild aural distress, turned down the volume. Visually the scene was indistinguishable from actually being physically present, although the total mimesis setting was again about six. Because the drone suppled visual data from a spherical visual field, she could turn her head and look up and down. Otherwise her spatial motion was restricted to the drone's autonomous movements.

Real-time responsive telepresence was possible, but only if the Supalite was hooked into the receiver and the drone directly controlled via the user's neural lace. Still, there were limits. Humanoid robot avatars were banned in humble territories, so the program had to extrapolate things like proprioreception. Haptics were pretty good but not perfect, despite claims otherwise. They gave the user a sometimes nauseating sensation of being within and without the experienced scene in a manner that just fell short of reality. This sensation was amplified when you lacked direct control of the host drone.

Then Sonya's face materialised above the rushing waters of the cataract. Cheyara, startled, opened her eyes and was catapulted back to her room. Almost swooning, she grabbed the side of the sink to steady herself. Sonya's face was still overlaid on the Nyuki scene, hanging over her unmade bed.

I'm not calling her, she thought.

But she did.

26TH AUGUST A.Y. 86

MISSION ELAPSED TIME: 2 Days.
LOCATION: MSAFIRI EN ROUTE TO NYUKI.

2 100, ship's time.

The Community News logo faded. Three willowy, gracile Taiyangren moved through the north embarkation zone of Abode 1. They were accompanied by five pink-hats, who hung behind despite their nominal role as shepherds. The Taiyangren propelled themselves forward in the weightless space, the crowd parting like the Red Sea before Moses.

Cheyara spotted three of the objectors mingling with the crowd. Two huddled together conversing whilst the third mouthed something at the Taiyangren. The sound was on mute so Cheyara couldn't hear what he said.

She unmuted.

'…the *Msafiri* Three surrendered themselves on arrival,' the voiceover said.

Great, Cheyara thought, watching the news in her cabin. *They have a name now.*

'There was some anger that the Three are not to be held, but the Sentinels judged them no danger to the community….'

A fourth Taiyangren was shown mounting the Council chamber steps. There was a closeup of a familiar, narrow, angular face on a slender neck. *Ibis N… Something.* She missed the name, the voiceover was too fast. Ey was followed by a gaggle of Abodans, most of whom were at least a head shorter than em. Some of the retinue was shouting and gesturing.

Ibis N Something passed close to the lens and Cheyara caught a flash of modified steel-grey irises contracting in the light. The camera followed the Taiyangren who shoved both doors of the council chamber open before striding through. Eir followers—pursuers?—piled in behind.

'The Ambassador is to meet with the objectors today.' The voiceover said, 'Negotiations are ongoing.'

'I bet they are.' Cheyara said to herself.

The next bit showed the interior of the council chamber. Several women filed down the aisle. It was post-sortition, so they were all new faces.

A speaker was gesticulating and shouting, calling for an immediate cessation of relations with the Taiyangren and the instant termination of the expedition. Murmurs of approval echoed in the chamber.

She'd seen enough.

'Off!'

The glowing window disappeared, and Cheyara was alone in the semi-darkness of her cabin. The only sound was the air circulation and her own breathing. The air she inhaled tasted stale and metallic. She lay on her berth, her thoughts whirling like dervishes. Retinal shapes danced on the ceiling. In an effort to calm her, the neural lace supplied images of sheep, leaping over a fence. Irritated, she put the lace on standby.

'Screw this!'

.

She sought company, climbing the ladder up the dimly lit Access Tunnel 2. The illuminating LEDS, mimicking a Nyuki heat day, emitted the yellowish colour of blood serum. Ascending the deep well, the 1 g acceleration of the *Msafiri* did funny things to her balance. More than once her foot slipped and adrenalin surged. Craning her neck she saw bright yellow, blue and red light flickering about three quarters of the way up the tunnel. Hearing an unfamiliar voice, she accelerated her ascent.

Dammit.

Her foot had slipped again.

The flickering lights were being cast from the half open crew-room hatch. Seven words were spoken, one every ten seconds or so. The voice spoke without particular inflection. She paused, listening and watching the moving light.

'Melt…Spring…Summer…Autumn…Freeze…Deep Winter.'

'Melt…Spring…Summer…Autumn…Freeze…Deep Winter.'

Cheyara peeped over the edge of the hatch and saw a familiar silhouette slumped in one of the couches. Heron sat behind a moving time-lapse 3D orrery projection of the

Asali system. Cheyara frowned, squinting to see beyond the bright simulation.

Heron's chest was caved and eir shoulders were lowered. Ey held a plastic bottle. Eir hair was down, obscuring cheekbones. The bright reflected colours of the orrery slid over the walls of the dimly-lit cabin.

Asali the yellow G type star flickered at the orrery's centre. A glowing red-orange ball shot around Asali, following an elliptical course. This was the red dwarf star Biloko. In real time it orbited Asali once every eight Earthian years, here accelerated to about sixty seconds per circuit. The voice recited the resulting seasons.

'Melt...Spring...Summer...Autumn...Freeze...Deep Winter.'

Deep winter for the furthest point of the orbit, when Biloko was at its furthest from Asali. Summer for when the red star made its closest approach to the parent star. By now, other facts were running through her mind. Biloko was a fraction as bright as the Earth's sun and its mass was just over one percent of the Earth's parent star. Nyuki, a tiny blue-green globe, circled Biloko once every 7.5 Terran days....

Heron was watching her and had already straightened up. Cheeks flushing, Cheyara smiled, pulling herself into the room and half-staggering across the deck. She arrested a fall by grabbing the side of the couch in which Heron sat. Heron was wearing a t-shirt and she could see the long, deep white scar encircling eir left, 'natural' forearm. This was anomalous, as both the Taiyangren and Abodans had the technology to stimulate full limb regeneration. She knew it was essentially a field repair.

Heron already had a hairband in eir hand and swept eir hair into the habitual ponytail.

The deep shadows cast by the projection emphasised eir bony, pallid face and thin lips. Two days into space-fall and it seemed to Cheyara that eir body was changing shape. Eir tight-fitting ochre flight suit hung differently on narrower shoulders, drawing attention to slightly fuller breasts. If she had to guess, then Cheyara would have said that Heron had chosen a strongly oestrogen-progesterone driven somatic expression for the expedition.

'Projection mute,' Heron said.

The mantra of seasons stopped. Heron nodded at the bottle that ey held in eir artificial hand.

'Want some?'

'Alcohol?'

'Yes.'

'That's forbidden.'

'Not until we make planetfall.'

Cheyara levered herself into an adjacent couch. She reached for the bottle, sucking on the nipple. The strong tang of whiskey went up her nose.

'Wow,' she said.

'Yes.'

Cheyara supposed that a super-charged Taiyangren liver, no doubt enhanced with nanotech or whatever, would deal with alcohol very efficiently. No cirrhosis, fatty liver syndrome or cancer for the Taiyangren. Maybe Heron was incapable of getting drunk.

Which would be sad.

'So now you tell me what's bothering you,' Heron said.

'I told you, nothing!'

'You know that I wasn't responsible.'

'What?'

'That I didn't summon them.'

'I never said you did.'

'We're all linked to the Taiyangren Cloud. They possibly found out that way.'

'You know what?' Cheyara said, 'It doesn't matter. The Consilience was broken. For the first time in sixty years, it was broken!' She paused, her voice ringing in the cabin. She was shocked at the volume of her own words.

'...And you're worried that the mission will be scrubbed....'

'Of course I am! Ramon was right. There had to be another way.'

'But not in the time. We had to launch.'

'But did we?'

'You know we did. Samudra....'

'Samudra be damned! You can't claim that the Zungui made us do it. That's consequentialist bullshit!'

Heron shrugged.

'Besides, no-one was hurt,' ey said.

'There's hurt, and there's hurt. They used force. You could have stopped them.'

'So could you.'

Heron sipped whiskey.

'My people did what was necessary. The lesser of two evils.'

'It was violence.'

'Which you can't always avoid.'

'We don't believe that.'

'Don't you?'

Before them, Nyuki circled Biloko and Biloko circled Asali. The pattern was robotic, unchanging, a product of the universal laws of gravitation. Celestial bodies compelled to repeat billion-year habits imposed upon them by vast, impersonal forces.

And what about us? Cheyara thought. Are we, too, doomed

to repeat destructive patterns imposed on us by vast, impersonal forces? Are we prisoners of our evolutionary past? Are we destined to fall?

She rubbed her eyes, feeling exhaustion settle on her like heavy snow. The early, euphoric days of this project seemed remote. Sonya, Samudra, the never-ending burden of responsibilities…. It was all too much. Her limbs felt like lead weights as she slumped in the couch. The tipsiness from the whiskey magnified her lassitude.

It's too late. This mission is tainted, and we haven't even made planetfall.

'Stop,' Heron said, pausing the orrery as the miniature Nyuki had begun its pass behind Biloko. From Cheyara's position, it looked as if the semi-eclipsed world was being consumed by red fire. She shivered, her skin creeping.

It seemed a little portentous for comfort.

7TH AUGUST A.Y. 86

MISSION ELAPSED TIME: 17 Days Before Launch. LOCATIONS: DWARF PLANET LENG TO ABODE 1. ORBITAL HABITAT.

She was in the main room in the dome on Leng when her recall order came. Azleena was with her. Cheyara relayed the news. Azleena smiled and they embraced. Cheyara found herself holding back tears.

'No time for a farewell party,' Azleena said, 'What the heck, I'll call the others. We'll have one tonight.'

'I'll pack first.'

While Cheyara was packing, she activated the Nyuki livestream. There were interference lines across the image, probably a solar storm on Biloko, but it was viewable. The forest was now a patchwork of green and grey-brown and the Matua stood outside the half-completed first floor of her wicker house. Three juvenile humbles with large black eyes and yellow-white fur were playing with mud at her feet. Their facial spiracles pulsed as they burbled. Two and a half months old and they were already beginning to talk.

The explosive rate of growth had been compared to the extinct elephant shrew of Earth. The biologists were still figuring out how the first hatchlings managed this in the relatively food-poor early spring forest. The currently favoured theory was that the Matua consumed a nutrient-rich form of 'sweet' perennial fungus that was common in the soil, converting it into aromatics and simple sugars in her honey-stomach.

But who really knew?

The Matua was regurgitating food now, visiting each juvenile and vomiting in their yawning mouths. After feeding, the children burbled with delight and went on playing with mud. She watched them for some minutes, totally absorbed. Despite the static, Cheyara almost felt as if she could reach out and touch the forest.

But not quite.

Soon, she thought, stomach frothing and heart thrumming. *Soon!*

.

Then she was aboard the shuttle.

The starlike point of Abode 1 was visible a good two hours before their arrival. Tired with endless orbital journeys, she willed the shuttle to go faster but unfortunately this did not have any effect on celestial mechanics.

The bright point resolved itself into a familiar tuna-can shape with a solar array disk at one end and heat radiators at the other. The space settlement was haloed by smaller starlike objects. Closer still, the structure of the smaller objects became discernible. One in particular caught her attention. From a distance, it was a crisscross of spiderwebs that glowed with rainbow colours. Cheyara activated the window magnifier to get a better look. The magnifier revealed a large, open network of trusses glowing with the artificial aurora of the radiation shield. Spacedock.

The *Msafiri* was one of three ships floating within, a stubby cylinder with two shuttle-blisters, attached to the scaffold by service umbilicals. The cylindrical hull was stealth-armoured in black to make it less visible from orbit. In just over two weeks, the ship would plunge into the inner Asali system with Cheyara and Heron onboard. Her skin tingled with anticipation.

A ship of Taiyangren design hung in a berth opposite the *Msafiri*. The craft resembled a shark with a smooth, seamless hull. Its cargo doors had folded themselves back, exposing a cavernous space and vague, silver-grey shapes moving within. The ship was large enough to be crewed, but had no windows. It didn't need any. The hull, which quivered a little as she watched, was dotted with millions of sensors, which a Taiyangren could utilise at will. The ship was about a third larger than the *Msafiri*, which resembled a docile herbivore beside the predatory lines of the Taiyangren vessel.

Passing the spacedock, the shuttle nosed close to Abode 1. Cheyara's seat provided a grandstand view of the rendezvous. The bulk of the stubby cylinder filled the curved window, spinning slowly on its axis. Her eye wandered over the rough, even surface of the shield-hull to the disk array of super-efficient solar panels that were positioned parallel to the northern face of the 'can.' The disk of solar panels matched the diameter of the habitat and was supported by the tubular north dock complex that stuck out from the centre of the tuna-can like a candle from the middle of a cake. The north dock's doors had swung open, anticipating their arrival.

After several hours glued to the seat, Cheyara was stiff, cramped and ready to move. Her fingers dug into a painful knot at the base of her neck that she'd acquired during sleep. The large-limbed woman next to her, an engineer she didn't know, was fidgeting.

The passengers buckled themselves in for the final approach. The shuttle spiralled towards its berth and Cheyara, her stomach churning, stifled her vomit reflex. She really was a rotten space-traveller. The woman next to Cheyara was still fidgeting in her seat. When she was finally released into the habitat she'd probably whoop and run a marathon.

There were multiple shudders and the green lights winked on, indicating a successful docking. Cheyara's neighbour muscled in front, taking prime position by the airlock. The other two passengers hung back with glazed expressions, their minds floating in the Community Cloud. Finally the lock opened with a hiss and they filed into the docking zone.

The embarkation zone was a large, pressurised annular cylinder that surrounded the berths. Today it was packed with busy people who drifted to and fro, pushing themselves along via handles that were evenly placed on the walls, or if they were overhead via an annular 'climbing frame' structure that ringed the zone. Accompanying the humans were robots that buzzed through the air on random but purposeful trajectories.

Some people were from Abode 1 and familiar to her, but others were not. These others no doubt hailed from one of the other Abode habitats. Six of these habitats shared a high orbit over Leng, the final two were in the inner Asali system.

A few of the visitors were probably tourists, visiting the founding habitat of the collective. That was probably the purpose of the small family just ahead who were dressed in bright, multicoloured clothes. The two children were fighting over a soft toy verdiphant.

Still in the main part of the zone, Cheyara spotted a Taiyangren couple up in the 'climbing frame,' recognisable by their various cybernetic implants and willowy, modified limbs. One of them looked heavily pregnant. They were both more heavily modified than Heron. One had a set of extra arms, each grafted under a shoulder.

Cheyara, her anthropologist's antennae twitching, noticed that most Abodans were avoiding the space in which the Taiyangren floated. One or two cast nervous glances in their direction. Despite an official philosophy of inclusion, many Abodans were wary of their neighbours.

Cheyara heard her name called and saw Magrena clinging to a handrail close to the exit corridor. She wore a blue outfit decorated with saffron symbols of her own design and dark blue snow boots. Her wiry, long white hair formed a frond-like halo around a deeply wrinkled face, puffy in the microgravity. One hundred and seven years old (not counting her time in the *Gun-Yu*'s freezer), Magrena had had multiple longevity treatments but refused cosmetic surgery. Perhaps this was because she was cultivating the image of a Wise Elder.

Or perhaps she just couldn't be bothered.

Magrena saw Cheyara and beckoned with a long finger.

'Good. You're here.' Her voice sounded adenoidal and her eyes watered. 'I feel like shit. I need gravity.' Cheyara floated close, manoeuvring her luggage as Magrena and she each grabbed a handle on the moving pathway that shot them down the long passage to the elevators. There was a crowd waiting at the elevators and Magrena shoved her way to the front, ignoring the odd comment and scowl. An elevator door opened and Magrena flung herself inside, almost colliding with the transparent wall. Cheyara stifled a smile. She gave the waiting people what she hoped was an apologetic expression and followed Magrena inside.

Another couple of people were already trying to enter the elevator, but Magrena waved them away.

'Council business.' She said.

'You're still just a citizen, Magrena.' a young man said. Magrena gave him a look and he shrank back from the doors. Cheyara settled in a seat by Magrena and the doors closed. Soon the elevator was descending into Abode 1.

'What?' Magrena said.

'Nothing.'

'Bullshit!'

'Sometimes, Magrena, you can be so…Earthian.'

The lift ground to a halt and the door slid open. Magrena grabbed a strap on Cheyara's luggage and yanked.

Cheyara didn't try to stop her, but hefted her second bag, which felt like lead in the Earth-level artificial gravity.

A car with council insignia was already opening its doors for them. Cheyara secured the luggage in the trunk as the car's rotors started to spin. Cheyara thought that flying such a short distance was a bit excessive, but said nothing.

They sat in the back, face to face. Magrena watched impassive as Cheyara fumbled with her seat belt. The car was already moving forward and Cheyara, facing the back of the car, felt the tug of her body against her restraints. The car sped for the council chambers.

The Abode 1 orbital space settlement was a standard tuna-can design with an internal radius of five hundred metres, rotated to provide Earth-strength gravity. The main habitation area was a strip along the inside of the cylinder that was landscaped with hills, lakes and roads. The hills were hollow, disguising living space, utilities and emergency shelters.

A translucent cylinder was positioned above the ground at a radius of about four hundred metres, blocking a clear view of the far side. This cylinder was composed of translucent sheets that were designed to mimic a cloudy sky. Its function was to scatter light, imported via a complex mirror system. The structure also controlled air movement and humidity, even simulating rain.

An inhabitant of the interior would see a hilly, park-like landscape curving up each side until obscured by the narrower 'sky' cylinder. Disk shaped red-brown walls on each side enclosed the cylinder, giving the space a slightly claustrophobic feel. This general arrangement was common to all six of the oldest Abode habitats.

The internal temperature of this, first habitat was kept at a subtropical twenty-five degrees. The landscape had been planted with a mixture of Mediterranean and African formal styles. The car now sped over the enclosed Great Park fringed by hillocks that disguised the University library, lectures halls, laboratories and offices.

The car flew through a flock of white doves. The display was pretty, and for a moment she forgot that it was only virtual. Below the flapping doves was the building-sculpture of Chuz Lee. Chuz Lee had been an artist-architect of the second generation. The construction had a shiny, liquid grey surface that undulated in the mirrored light of the artificial sky. It was the sculpture in which Sonya and she had got lost one happy day, seven long years ago.

Why did it have to end so atrociously, Cheyara wondered. She thought back over their roller-coaster relationship, unable quite to pinpoint where things had gone so spectacularly wrong. Maybe if she'd had more wit, or tact, or honesty, at the exact moment of schism, then she'd still be with Sonya. Or maybe not. Some couplings are too incandescent to ever really last.

Now they flew over the council complex, adjacent to the University. The complex, which featured a main street lined with secondary administrative buildings, exchange centres, cafés, a mosque, a church and a buddhist temple, was known informally and inaccurately as the 'Capital.' Their destination was the main council building situated in the centre of the 'Capital.'

The main building was composed of terracotta blocks and had been deliberately built above ground for visibility. The square in front of the main doors of the council chamber was occupied. The car circled. Cheyara looked down. A robot sentinel hovered below them, keeping a vigil over the objectors.

Forty people stood in the square, each taking their place on a human grid that faced the council chambers. Each wore a long white silver-brocaded robe that piled at their feet. As the car moved overhead, each oval began to move. Heads turned in unison, faces angling up, as if propelled by tropism. Cheyara's skin prickled as forty pair of eyes locked on the car. Each head was topped by an immaculate black quiff. Each face was identical. Every one wore the same, blank stare.

One of the protesters on the front row reached upwards, passing a gloved hand over their face. Then Cheyara was looking straight into the eyes of her ex. Of course, she *would* be there, at that moment. Greeting the traitor. Sonya remained as expressionless as her companions. She thrust out her chest. Her golden hair cascaded over her shoulders.

Fuck.

Cheyara's scalp prickled and her face flushed. All of a sudden she wanted to shut herself away in a small dark space and take the foetal position and never again emerge.

'Just ignore them,' Magrena said as the car hovered over the landing pad on the roof. From her position, Cheyara could now only see the tops of objectors's heads. She could still see a patch of blonde in the front row. As she watched, the blonde patch vanished, replaced by a quiff identical to the others. Sonya had made her point, and was now, once more, one of the collective. Individual objectors changed, but the display remained. Together they'd occupied the square for two thousand, four hundred and seventy seven days.

The car wobbled a little and descended, touching down lightly on the roof. The vehicle's rotors slowed and stopped. Cheyara suddenly felt heavy. She'd become used to the extreme buoyancy of Leng, despite a daily dose of Terran gs in the base centrifuge. The car doors hissed open and Magrena had already unbuckled herself. She hobbled out, followed by Cheyara. They were on a roof top terrace, surrounded by a lush forest of potted plants. There was even a hammock strung between two date palms. Cheyara suspected that many of the plants had been placed there at Magrena's insistence. Sonorous chants echoed from the square below.

'REMEMBER! REMEMBER! REMEMBER!'

'As if we'd forget,' Magrena snorted. 'As if *I'd* forget,' she muttered, pushing the exit door open.

·

Their footsteps rang on brick steps. At the bottom of the stairway was a short corridor that led to a mezzanine overlooking the now-empty council chambers. Abode's flag hung on the walls over the chambers, eight silver stars surrounding a silver coin against a sky-blue background. A symbol of settlement.

Magrena opened a door at the end of the mezzanine, ushering Cheyara into a small windowless room that was decorated with mosaics showing tropical islands floating in Earthian oceans. The room was bedecked with many potplants placed in passive-aggressive positions. A circular table filled most of the room, ringed with chairs. All but two of the chairs were occupied by the other eight people who composed the Nyuki Special Committee. Fortunately, there was at least one friendly face.

Heron Y Mouse sat on the far side of the table, upright, poised, professional, alert. Heron nodded acknowledgment to Cheyara, pointing to the empty seat beside eir. Cheyara squeezed her way along the small space between the back of occupied seats and the wall, upsetting one fern that wobbled on a thin column. She only just stopped the column from toppling.

Finally, she reached her seat.

Heron smiled and they exchanged greetings. Magrena had already taken her chair and was whispering to a thin woman named Agara. Cheyara didn't like it: the exchange looked uncomfortably conspiratorial.

'What is it?' She said. Both women looked at her.

'We've something to tell you,' Magrena said.

No shit!

'I advised against disclosure….' Agara said.

'But…,' Cheyara said.

'But we think there's been a leak,' Agara said. 'We think that everyone's going to know, soon. We think….'

'Besides, Heron dissented,' Magrena said. 'Ey insisted that we tell you immediately. And since the information we're about to disclose is of Taiyangren origin, we felt that we had no right to refuse that request.'

'Thank you.' Heron said.

'Heron?' Agara said.

'You recall the justification for Expedition One?' Heron said.

Cheyara nodded.

'Yes.'

'Why the non-intervention policy was broken?'

'Yes…. It was technical…. An AI recommendation….'

'Do you recall the specifics?'

Cheyara shrugged.

'I can just tell you what everybody knows.'

'And what does everybody know?' Said Magrena.

'That the grace period that was bought for us has a high probability of being of finite length, given what we know about the Zungui, but….'

'But?' Heron said.

'But the risk of an incursion's pretty small per calendar year, isn't it? Something like point zero one in a hundred….'

She shuffled her feet, cowering under their collective stare.

'Still, we know that the Zungui are committed to total colonisation….' She said.

'So their efforts to settle new systems will never stop,' Magrena said.

'Which means that they'll get here eventually no matter what, I suppose….' Cheyara said. 'But the numbers….'

She struggled to recall the specific data.

'The numbers the simulations produced to justify Expedition One suggested possible arrival times that were still reasonably distant….' Heron said.

'But not so distant that they justified the continued quarantine of Nyuki,' Agara said.

'And those estimates,' Heron said, 'Were based on the best data available…at the time.'

'So what's changed?'

'Image play,' Magrena said and the lights dimmed as the first photograph materialised over the tabletop's centre. This persisted for a few seconds before being replaced by another. The image sequence showed what she thought at first might be a stellar cluster: a scattering of tiny bright specks on black, salt on velvet. These distant shots were replaced by closeups showing a group of blurry silver-grey objects. Each subsequent image showed more objects in the cloud.

'Couldn't you get a higher resolution?'

'We're working on it.'

'What took these?'

'One of our probes,' Heron said.

In the next photo, four of the objects were emitting bright bluish light. Cheyara's skin began to crawl. The image would have been transmitted by Supalite, so it would have been received almost in real time.

'Where was this taken?' Her throat had tightened and it was an effort to force out the words.

'The next system. NGS 578128.'

'The Samudra system,' Cheyara said, blinking rapidly, 'So the rumours are true.'

There was a moment of silence. Then Magrena and Agara nodded, simultaneously.

'That's only three light years away!' Cheyara said. 'How long have you known?'

'The Taiyangren only told us six months ago,' Magrena said, staring at Heron.

Cheyara glanced at Heron and their eyes met. Eir face remained unreadable in the dim light. Cheyara's thoughts whirled. With the Zungui next door, no wonder the Taiyangren had insisted on Expedition Two.

'But we have a few years,' Cheyara said, hugging herself. 'By the look of that activity, it's not that advanced....'

'That's not the point,' Heron said, shaking eir head. 'Zungui seed replicators issue from a single point of origin. You know that. If they're in the adjacent system, then we know for certain they've changed their target strategy.'

'And the outcome for a target system is always the same....' Cheyara said, suddenly conscious of the sweat trickling down her temples. She gasped, feeling smothered. Closing her eyes, she forced herself to take deep breaths.

'Yes,' Heron was saying, 'The seed arrives, activates. They spread....'

'...Consuming the target system.' Magrena said.

'Total colonisation.' Agara said, nodding. Cheyara

winced. *Colonisation.* She hated that poisonous, Earthian word. But in this case, it was accurate.

'Total colonisation,' Magrena repeated. She had not taken her eyes off the last image, which still hung in the air. They were just blue-grey blobs in darkness, a million light-years removed from the four horsemen of Judaeo-Christian myth. They remained a grim portent of apocalypse.

Heron reached out and took Magrena's hand.

Kin in suffering, Cheyara thought.

'How long?' she said, in a very small voice.

'If we're unlucky,' Agara said, 'A handful of years. Maybe even less. Depends upon the speed of the colonisation wavefront.'

'And Zungui seed replicators are one kilogram or less,' Heron said, 'And they're undetectable.'

'What about the magnetic sails they use, for deceleration? Wouldn't we see them?' Agara said. She'd clearly been doing her homework.

Heron shook eir head.

'Unfortunately, they jettison them long before arrival, and they're also undetectable, at least at interstellar distances. Believe me, we've looked.'

'So….' Cheyara said.

'They might be here already.'

The lights came up and the physical images faded, but remained etched on Cheyara's consciousness.

They might be here already.

'We must act,' Agara said, 'As if they're not. As if we still have time.'

'Oh, come on!' Magrena said.

'She's right,' Heron said. 'What other choice have we?'

Cheyara thought of her brother and sister, of the two squabbling children she'd seen in the embarkation zone, of the new world the three Abode generations had worked so hard to build. Their plans, their hopes, their ambitions now counted for nothing.

The future had just been erased.

5TH SEPTEMBER A.Y. 86

MISSION ELAPSED TIME: 12 Days.
LOCATION: MSAFIRI EN ROUTE FOR NYUKI.

They'd been negotiating for ten days.

Magrena kept her updated as Cheyara no longer had the heart to watch the community news. That wouldn't have told her much, anyway. The objectors, the Taiyangren Ambassador Ibis N Antelope and a council representative now sat around a table in a closed room in the Abode 1 Council chambers for fifteen hours each day. The doors were shut to everyone when the meeting was in session.

'They don't even stop for meals,' Magrena said, describing how a food synthesiser had been provided for the meeting on the third day. The Community News drones hovered outside the room, waiting to pounce whenever someone emerged for the lavatory or bed. The negotiators wouldn't say a word.

But as Magrena said, it wasn't hard to guess the parameters of the dispute. The objectors would be pushing for the immediate cancellation of Expedition 2. Ibis would have vetoed this, citing the potentially imminent arrival of the Zungui as justification. The Council representative would be caught in the middle. Officially, they'd have to support the expedition—which given the dangers facing everyone seemed like common sense to Cheyara. Still, opposing a minority pledge was seen by many as anti-Consilience. And right now the Council was doing everything it could to avoid another wave of possibly violent protest. So who knew which way the Council would eventually swing.

Magrena called it an 'Earthian standoff.'

·

Unable to bear the tension, Cheyara practised avoidance. This was easier than she expected as the *Msafiri* was closing in on Nyuki. That day, Cheyara spent some time inspecting its surface features through the telescope in the observation lounge. The world was frustrating to observe because of the extensive cloud cover. Still, from this distance, you could see the play of auroral light at the poles, the result of Nyuki's powerful electromagnetic field. This, plus extensive cloud cover, provided protection from dangerous stellar eruptions on Biloko.

Every so often the clouds would break and she'd glimpse a deep blue ocean surface dotted with gigantic icebergs, a pattern of islands, the curving edge of a green subcontinent, a jutting peninsula. In those moments, the world seemed close enough to taste.

Later, she summoned the orrery, expanding the Nyuki portion of the image. She found it satisfying to run her finger along the timeline, watching the rapid succession of the seasons in accelerated time. Nyuki was fated to endure a binge-purge cycle of heat and cold over its eight year orbit. The planet was an icy ball when its parent star Biloko was at aphelion in Deep Winter but in the Melt season a rapid and dizzying change happened as the ice-shell melted. By midsummer, temperatures in the temperate zones could be as high as subtropical. After the 'summer solstice' the planet would begin its orbital retreat and Autumn would come, followed by Freeze season when the whole planet was once more cocooned in ice.

So she ran her finger across the timeline, the oceans morphing from white to grey to blue and back again. In sped-up time, the continents emerged from shells of ice, frost and snow, their surfaces exploding into rich, deep greens. In autumn the forest-cover turned yellow-brown and then the white returned. Melt, Spring, Summer: ice to emerald. Summer, Autumn, Freeze: emerald to brown-gold to ice. On a continental scale, at least.

Reams of fresh video and full immersive footage had been tagged to the orrery since she'd last looked. Although she'd intensively studied the Nyuki datastreams, there was such a quantity of new material that she could never fully assimilate it all. This was positive, in a way. It meant that there was always something new on the map.

Scenes from the recent Melt were a favourite. One clip was taken from a drone hovering about ten thousand metres up in the stratosphere. The video showed breaks in blossoming thunderheads. Far below was the steel-grey, undulating surface of the ocean, with icebergs to the horizon.

Another video, from the equatorial zone, was from the perspective of a drone skimming over the ocean's surface. The drone flew over large, algal patches, zipping past flocks of flying animals hovering over the water. The later part of the video showed tantalising shadows suggestive of shoals of fish and larger marine animals moving beneath the sea.

Some of the most spectacular images had been taken when the drones approached the landmasses. The drones encountered vast fields of ice and then mountainous glaciers that were in the process of calving sediment-laden icebergs.

Images from remote drones flying over land revealed dark blue pools of water on glacial surfaces, presaging sliding ice and explosive calving.

These images were somewhat misleading. Viewed from afar, on rare cloudless days, Nyuki's polar caps remained comparatively large, even at midsummer. Polar and mountain glaciers would only retreat a certain amount over the warm period. The warm period, after all, lasted only a couple of Earthian years, compared to Deep Winter's six. The changes in heat balance over Melt, Spring and Summer were enough to cause some glacial ablation and end-melting, but not to thaw the poles. So most of the ice on the seas in Melt and Spring was drifting pack ice. This was despite balmy summer climates at the tropics and equatorial regions.

After a while, footage of ice and oceans became monotonous. In many ways she preferred the videos taken on the land. The global map even had vintage videos from the first years of exploration. She found a clip from the first ever season of robotic surveys on Nyuki. On the last days of melt, drones had arrived on a peninsula that jutted from the third Australia-sized landmass in the southern hemisphere. At first they flew over bare rock and grey soil. Then a large array of grey rough-surfaced cylinders with recognisable root buttresses loomed from the mist. In between the boles were dotted calcified structures resembling corals or leafless bushes.

At first, the video commentary stated, the watching researchers had thought that it was a fossil forest. They were soon proved wrong. Cue closeups of grey-green shoots sprouting from the top of the trunks. And within days, the rapid greening of the continents had begun. As the last ice melted, the forests grew rapidly.

A classic time-lapse of one northern-hemisphere forest showed the growth of a day compressed into three minutes. This one gave her a buzz of nostalgia: she'd first seen it at school. In the first seconds you could see the unfurling of leaves, the bursting of buds and the opening of flowers. Cryobark was rapidly shed from tree trunks as branches grew and trunks shuddered.

Later videos in the old sequence showed animals. Insects burst from winter cocoons, struggling out of the soil, wriggling legs, snapping pincers and fluttering wings. Vertebrate animals pushed aside clods of earth and scuttled over bare, grey earth. Flying creatures that were not quite birds and not quite downy bats emerged from woven sacs that were hidden in the cavities of what were soon dubbed umbrella trees.

Larger animals emerged from burrows, avian-mammal forms the size of hedgehogs, rabbits and badgers. They clawed their way into the yellow-red light, sniffing the chill air. Then the largest animals appeared from hibernation places in caverns and dens. These included herbivorous chlorelles, verdiphants and predatory vespons.

At the end of the last Melt, when she'd still been on Leng, a drone had penetrated deep into caves at the roots of the mountains on Northern Subcontinent 2. The machine had discovered a cavern refuge of cocooned herbivores. Each cocoon was translucent brown and shaped like a flattened, ridged, oversized egg. She knew that the cocoons were made of a form of glycoprotein that was exuded by the animal in the early stages of the hibernation process, which hardened to form a protective shell.

The herbivores in question were identified as striped chlorelle, medium-sized browsers that inhabited the spring and summer forests. In hibernation the stilt like, multi-jointed legs were folded neatly against the trunk as the animal reposed in a foetal position inside the cocoon.

The reawakening began with one animal in the warmest corner of the cave. An infrared view showed the lead animal's core temperature rise from a cold purple-blue to orange-red as internal metabolic fires were stoked. The biological warming spread like a contagion through the cave, which was soon full of twitching, jerking animals. Hind legs kicked, deforming then breaking the hardened, gelatinous seal of their cocoons.

Wrists flexed and hooves kicked. Eyelids fluttered, the cavern echoing with pants and groans as the animals struggled into motion. The first attempts to stand resembled the clumsy motion of newborns. Forelimbs shuddered and bodies rolled as the animals pushed themselves up from the stone floor. Falls were not uncommon.

The chlorelle had 'ruffs' that extended around the neck, membranes supported by fingers of bone. Once the animals had discarded their cocoons, the ruffs flexed like thin, webbed hands.

At first the chlorelle herd milled in the cavern, until bellwether animals discovered the exit and they began to file through the passage that led to the surface. As they trooped they disturbed flitters that fluttered amongst the stalactites as the moaning, lowing herd picked their way up the rocky slope to the entrance, their ruffs fully opening in the sunlight.

On emergence, the membranes between the fingers were mostly green tinged-grey. In the sunlight, the algae that lived symbiotically within would reproduce and by late spring the ruffs would have turned a livid green.

She felt sure that Sonya and the other objectors had also watched this video, which had over 10 million views.

Why else had they decided to carve the pledge in the shape of a chlorelle?

.

Then she went for a virtual walk on the beach. This was possible because they'd been permitted to land robotic avatars on the shores of Southern Subcontinent 3, which lacked language and tool using intelligent life.

In the foreground, triple-tusked undulus moved up the grey-and-brown shingle, extending their head and shoulders forward, then humping their pelvis in a movement that echoed extinct Earthian seals. From afar they looked like giant slate-grey caterpillars, their sirenian moans carrying on cold drafts. In the distance, glacier icebergs calved into the sea, joining a drift of blue and green ice-mountains that extended to the horizon. Above her large, marine flitters sailed on katabatic winds.

The haptics on the avatar were of high quality and she turned the mimesis level up to nine, but staggered in the icy blasts. The avatar almost toppled in a gust more than once and her face was soon numb. Eventually, she crouched, touching the shingle with synthetic fingertips. The stones were cold and the shore had a characteristic, almost familiar smell. The aromatics of the algal enzyme molecule behind the scent apparently differed from those of Earth, but only Magrena's generation would have known the difference.

Then the world went blank, and for a moment she was falling through nothingness. She was back in the observation room, with a message flashing across her visual field.

ERROR: TRANSMISSION INTERRUPTED

She blinked the message away and rubbed her chilled arms. Her teeth chattered and her ears, nose, fingers and toes had gone numb from the cold. Except that she'd never really *been* cold. The illusion had been so real that the cold receptors in her skin had fired, causing vasoconstriction. It was a form of hypnotic suggestion.

The real Nyuki was visible in the observation window, a bright visible disk. She could see greenish illuminations at both poles. The volatile Biloko was obviously having another of its tantrums.

She was suddenly tired of synthetic experience. A mimesis level of nine—even ten—was not life. The difference might be imperceptible to the senses and the rational mind, but it was felt in the gut. There was always something off about it, at the holistic level. Despite her numb toes, she'd never stood on the surface of Nyuki. The avatar offered only a proxy knowing. She needed directly to touch the soil, breathe the air, smell the odour of the forest. To hell with avatars.

'Hi.'

She jumped.

Heron had materialised in the lounge and she hadn't even noticed. But somehow the timing was right.

'What is it?'

'I just heard. They've made a decision. They'll be an announcement in half an hour.'

Cheyara nodded, following Heron out of the observation lounge. Her heart throbbed in her throat, and all her fingers and toes were crossed.

21ST AUGUST A.Y. 86

MISSION ELAPSED TIME: 3 Days before launch.
LOCATIONS: ABODE 1 TO MSAFIRI IN SPACEDOCK.

Two Bobbys were looking in at her when the blinds lifted.

Good thing I'm dressed, she thought, closing her suitcase and placing it on the floor by her bed. She resisted the urge to bare her bottom at her onlookers.

She left the room.

The lounge and the kitchen were empty. Her brother Leyon was still in the 'capital' on the other side of the habitat and her sister was presumably still asleep. Cheyara switched on the Community News channel in the kitchen then ordered a breakfast shake of chocolate-flavoured protein and a black coffee. The first item was news of a riot in Abode 1's 'capital.'

It had started as a protest the previous night. A crowd of concerned citizens filing down the main avenue of the complex. No-one seemed to know when it had turned nasty. The news showed images of the crowd running wild, smashing windows, hurling objects, screaming, shouting. She recognised many of them. Friends and colleagues with contorted, leering faces.

One clip showed the square in front of the council chambers. Robed figures were running two and fro like frightened cats. The Sentinels had immobilised some rioters, but there were too many to stop completely. They showed one Sentinel battered on the ground. Two people she knew smashed another against a wall. People were trampled and had to be taken to hospital. Tranquillity Teams were sent out, but they were few and the rioters were many.

She watched in horror as weeping witnesses came before the camera and described what they had witnessed.

'Why are they doing this? Why!' one witness said to camera. One side of his face was heavily bruised.

Midway through the report, she was messaging Leyon, but of course there was no reply. He'd volunteered on the Tranquillity Team, and would no doubt be in the thick of it. She hoped that he was safe. She'd never seen anything like this before.

The Zungui, she thought, *the Zungui's driving people crazy.*

But she knew that wasn't totally true. She recalled the history of Abode. The craziness had been there all along. A symptom of their confinement, perhaps. So the Zungui were just catalysts.

The rest of the news was equally grim. Abodes 7 and 8 had decided unilaterally to collaborate on a starship, for evacuation. Some idiot was spouting apocalyptic nonsense on the Community Cloud. And the Council was promising regular sweeps of the Asali system for Zungui seed replicators.

She switched off the channel and ate breakfast in silence before leaving the house. The Bobbys did not follow her.

She walked up the path past the miniature lake. The local boys were still fishing for tilapia and waved at her before returning their attention to the water. The peaceful scene belied the chaos unfolding just a few hundred metres away, on the other side of the sky.

The church stood at the end of the path in a grove of eucalyptus. The building was octagonal with a conical roof. Its stained glass windows were simple geometric patterns in mauve, purple and pale yellow, reflecting the morning light of the cylindrical synthetic sky. The conical roof was surmounted by a crystal sphere about the size of a basket ball. Within the sphere a miniature barred spiral galaxy revolved at a leisurely pace.

The church had been built using eucalyptus wood from a design of her grandfather's, who had died eighteen years before she was born. When they'd been growing up the family had been regularly subjected to videos of the construction. Their father, who'd completed the project, had insisted this was a 'part of their heritage.' He spoke of a time when the clearing had been a building site pervaded by the scent of cut wood and the sound of sawing and plaining. Her grandfather had eschewed printed materials and robots, saying that the church would only be real if they could build it with their own hands. The sphere that surmounted the church had been made after completion, in her grandmother's workshop at home.

There were three Bobbys waiting for her, sitting on the church steps. Their long, white robes with silver brocade letters spilt over the bottom step, onto the grass. The silver letters on their robes spelt 'REMEMBER' in five hundred languages.

She hesitated when she saw them, not wanting to be followed. Then she thought, what does it matter?

Three identical blood stains spread over the Bobby's chests when she approached. The stains resembled Rorschach blots. She ignored the display and ducked around the side of the church.

The memorial garden at the back was a grid of black and grey obelisks of variable sizes. The family memorial was towards the rear. There were five names inscribed on the black obelisk. Reading bottom to top, there was one for mum and one for dad. The last three were for her grandparents of the Settler generation.

There was no named fourth grandparent because her mother's mother had used artificial insemination. This was in part due to the scarcity of males in the Settler generation. Cheyara's only known grandfather, Kwame, had been a child when he'd emerged from cryosleep. So was his eventual life partner, Cheyara's grandmother, Unyime.

All three grandparents had eventually succumbed to cancer: even Unyime, who had clung on to the ripe old age of 91. The disease was a legacy of thirteen years, ship time, on ice in the *Gun-Yu*'s cryosleep chambers. (Thirteen years on the *Gun-Yu*, travelling at relativistic speeds, but nine-hundred and ninety two years by an Earthian frame of reference). Anyway that, and a subsequent lifetime of exposure to cosmic rays in the orbit of Leng. None of her grandparents had been gene-edited for hard radiation environments and despite epigenetic therapy they had apparently lacked Magrena's iron constitution. Or more likely, her Taiyangren connections.

There were fresh flowers at the foot of the memorial, presumably placed by her sister. Cheyara knelt before the obelisk, offering a prayer to the Universe. Then she stood and turned to leave.

·

Later, she met her big sister Ayanna in the garden of their house. Fortunately, there were no Bobbys in sight. The garden was fringed by silver trees underplanted with proteas and ornamental grasses. Pleasantly-scented freesias, hoheria and clivia grew in the flowerbeds. Butterflies fluttered above the flowers. Cheyara and Ayanna sat on the lawn and watched the leaves of the silver trees wave in the winds kicked up by the uneven heating of the interior of Abode 1.

It was encouraging that her sister was finally outside. Ever since the news of the Zungui had broken she'd been holed up in her room. Leyon had asked Cheyara to keep a discrete eye on their sister whilst he was away.

An anomaly of acoustics and air circulation allowed them to hear faintly the cries of the protestors on the other side of the habitat.

Her sister seemed not to notice the sounds. There were hollows in Ayanna's cheeks and her neck looked too thin to support the weight of her head. Cheyara reached out and stroked her sister's hair.

'You need to eat more.'

Ayanna shuffled her feet, avoiding her sister's gaze.

'That's what Leyon says.'

'I'm sorry I have to go away.'

'It's okay.'

They sat silently side by side for while. A frog emerged from the undergrowth, hopping into the swimming pool with a plop.

'I wish….' Ayanna said, then lapsed into silence. The frog did a breast-stroke to the bottom of the pool. Cheyara wondered whether she should retrieve it, then smiled at the folly. Like the butterflies, the frog was a digital ornament, without material substance. She flipped her neural lace to standby and the ornaments vanished.

The distant cries continued.

'I wish I was going with you,' Ayanna said suddenly. 'I'd like to see real forests. Mum once showed me some old videos, from the Earth Archive. You won't believe how big the Amazon was, before they chopped it down and it all turned to desert.'

'Sometimes, I go and sit in the eucalyptus copse at night. I listen to the owl. I hear the rustle of the leaves and the frogs in the lake and the crickets in the bushes. I close my eyes and imagine what the forests were like on Earth, before the men destroyed them.'

Cheyara was rather surprised. That was the most she'd heard her sister say since she'd arrived. She hugged her tight.

'I'll walk in the forests for you,' she said and her sister smiled for the first time in weeks.

A notification materialised in Cheyara's visual field.

'I have to go. Say goodbye to Leyon.'

They embraced.

·

The car arrived ten minutes later. She put her suitcase in the trunk then sat in a passenger seat. The doors hissed closed and the AI started the rotors. The five Bobbys standing in front of their house watched the ascent of the taxi. The trip was a hop, over the hollow hills of the residential areas, but delivered her to an elevator where Magrena was waiting.

Magrena was wearing a frown.

'We have a serious problem,' she said, as the elevator doors opened.

Somehow Cheyara wasn't at all surprised.

·

There were seven of them.

Seven for each year since his death, Cheyara thought when she entered the *Msafiri*'s cargo hold. They were all undisguised. Her jaw-muscles tightened when she saw the identity of their spokesperson.

Sonya saw Cheyara enter and stopped mid-sentence,

her hair floating like straw-coloured waterweed in the microgra3vity. She'd been talking to two pink-hatted Tranquillity Team negotiators, whom Cheyara recognised as Ramon and Maya. Three spherical Sentinel robots hovered above them like judging angels. Their presence momentarily distracted Cheyara from the object that Sonya was holding in her hands. A small wooden carving of a chlorelle.

It was a second or two before the import of the carving hit home.

Oh, no.

The other six objectors were positioned in different places around the chamber. Four had wedged themselves in various places on the walls. Two perched on a cargo container. Counting Sonya, Cheyara recognised three of them from her student days. The others were strangers.

Heron had already crossed to the partition that cut the hold in two. This was a sealed transparent bulkhead with an airlock in the middle. On the airlock door was a yellow sign with a biohazard symbol above the words WARNING: STERILE ENVIRONMENT.

Ey passed eir fingertips along the periphery of the airlock, then caught Cheyara's eye. Cheyara inclined her head. It looked intact to her, too.

Through the bulkhead three storage containers were visible, destined for Nyuki's surface, after shuttle transport. At the far end of the sealed section, half hidden by shadow, was the flier that would be their surface transport. None of those items would be easy to replace, in the event of sabotage.

'You can't go,' Sonya said, looking at her, over the negotiator's shoulder. 'We won't let you.'

'But why?' Cheyara said.

'You know why. "The right of all forms of life to live is a universal right which cannot be quantified." That's in the Consilience, and it includes autonomy, yes? You used to know that.'

'I still do.'

'Then leave them alone. We can't allow what happened on Earth to happen on Nyuki. Ever.'

'You don't know what happened on Earth.' Magrena said, who'd entered the chamber behind them.

'If we do nothing,' Cheyara said, 'The Zungui will come and the humbles will be destroyed....'

'Reduced to data patterns.' Magrena said, 'Don't you care?'

'Of course we care. But that's irrelevant. Two wrongs....'

'Don't make a right. Okay. But at least they'd have a chance of survival, with us.'

'Survival as what? Exhibits in a reservation settlement in some other star system? That sounds like a living death to me.'

Sonya swept a hand over her body, and an emaciated humble with a milky-cataract eye and deep, puckered scars floated in the cargo hold. Behind Cheyara, one of the pink-hats caught their breath.

'That's not inevitable,' Cheyara said, 'there might be other ways....'

The humble glared at her, its rheumy eye weeping.

'It's the likely outcome and you know it.' The voice was hoarse, but for Cheyara the illusion was broken. Humbles didn't speak through their mouths. The *ersatz* humble was still grasping the carving.

Still, if the Zungui came, then Sonya was probably right. But it would be the best they could do, in evil circumstances. Cheyara bit her lip.

'We need to move towards understanding.' Ramon said.

Humble-Sonya brandished the carving.

'No.'

So there was nothing they could do.

Cheyara left the cargo hold, followed by Heron and Magrena. They floated in Access Tunnel 1, out of earshot of the objectors and the Sentinels.

'We've got some time,' Heron said, 'The launch window opens in fifty-five hours. Maybe your negotiators can work a compromise.'

Magrena snorted.

'Sonya won't budge,' Cheyara said. 'None of them will budge.'

'You could easily remove them.'

'We can't. You saw what she was carrying.'

'The carving?'

'Yes. It's a pledge.'

'What's a pledge?'

'A safeguard,' Magrena said, 'Against the tyranny of the majority. Under the Consilience, it can only be invoked in extreme circumstances by an injured party who lacks power. A pledge prohibits any action until the dispute is resolved. And resolution's mostly up to the injured party.'

'I see.' Heron said.

'I have to return to Abode,' Magrena said. 'You two, stay here.'

'And do what?' Cheyara said.

'Exactly what you'd do if this little problem didn't exist.' Magrena said, moving in the direction of the aft airlocks.

Easier said than done, Cheyara thought.

But she followed Magrena's advice.

23RD SEPTEMBER A.Y. 86

MISSION ELAPSED TIME: 30 Days.
LOCATION: MSAFIRI'S SHUTTLE IN NYUKI ORBIT.

In theory, she should have been happy. They'd made it to Nyuki orbit without mission cancellation. But of course, there were strings attached.

With Sonya, there were always strings.

Clad in a sterile flight suit, Cheyara joined Heron in the cramped cargo hold of the large shuttle. They were approaching the flier, which had been transferred to the shuttle the previous night.

She clung to the rails all the way as the floor pitched downwards. The shuttle had already detached itself from the *Msafiri* and was following a trajectory that would very soon be entering Nyuki's upper atmosphere. The deck under her feet was vibrating as the shuttle decelerated. The air in the hold was stifling and trickles of sweat poured down her face. They were leaving in a period that mimicked a so-called 'red day,' so the deck was bathed in red-orange light.

They climbed on board the flier and the canopy began to close over them. She fastened her webbing and glanced at Heron, who smiled. Once more, they were passengers. The initial flight of the flier, to Basecamp, was preprogrammed. The varicoloured display was playing over the dashboard. Cheyara's heart throbbed in her ears and her stomach was doing acrobatic tumbles. This time, she'd deactivated her personal visual launch countdown. Numbers scrolling in her face would only increase the tension.

Ey was looking at her.

'What's the problem?' Heron said.

'Nothing…it's just…. You know we'll be cancelled at the drop of a hat. They'll be watching, waiting for us to screw up.'

'Then we'd better not screw up,' Heron said.

'Easier said than done.'

'I'm sure you'll do your best.'

'Don't I always?' Cheyara said.

To distract herself she ran over the flight procedures. Most of it amounted to *sit tight while the flier AI does the work*. Then the canopy was sealed and the bay doors opened, admitting light and ferocious winds. The flier bucked slightly, but held fast to its rail. Its engines fired and rotor blades hummed like giant bees. The flier slid down to the end of the rail and there was a perceptible lurch as the rotors adjusted to free flight. Above them the shuttle accelerated and for a few moments Cheyara watched its soaring ascent with an unexpected melancholy.

Below them, the southern tip of Northern Subcontinent 2 was obscured by cloud. The flight program had them bank and descend in slow spirals. The flier shuddered as they entered the turbulent, misty, white zone of a cloud bank. They sank, emerging a few minutes later below the cloud deck.

Then they were flying over swampy wetland, a vast delta formed from the millions of tonnes of water that flowed from the mountains in immense cataracts each Melt. Cheyara looked down at the silvery-blue arteries that flowed through yellow-green vegetation. She was glad that they wouldn't have to navigate through that terrain; the humbles' forest was situated on elevated ground.

A few minutes later they came to the periphery of the wetlands, marked by a region of patchy, grass-like cover on low hummocks. For a while they followed the course of a river which cut through the trees on its way to the delta. The forest was a sea of vibrant green, clear to the mountains that fringed the horizon. The flier parted from the river, levelling off and speeding over treetops. Their heading was in the general direction of the mountains.

Cheyara was surprised—shocked was a better word—at the extent and vigour of the growth that she saw below her. All this and the forest was still half grown, with many plants struggling from the damp grey soil. The growth was driven by the planet's approach to Asali, which was still far from its peak insolation. Still, the territory below the shuttle was solid tree-cover over rolling hills.

'Are you ready for this?' Heron's voice was amplified by her ear implants.

It's a bit late if I'm not, Cheyara thought, as they sped towards the Basecamp. The forest below reminded her of Ayanna and she hoped that her sister was watching the flier feed. A gut feeling told her that she almost certainly would be. Here was a forest that matched the ones from the past of the now-consumed Earth.

And within decades, it might all be gone.

24TH AUGUST A.Y. 86

MISSION ELAPSED TIME: 0.125 Days before launch.
LOCATION: MSAFIRI IN SPACEDOCK.

Cheyara gave up practising the humble language. Her throat was sore and on audio playback her efforts sounded squeaky and embarrassing.

It was all pointless, anyway. Until the dispute was resolved, they were stuck in spacedock. Magrena hadn't been in touch for twenty-four hours.

There was a knock and Heron poked eir head around the cabin door.

'You'd better do that up,' ey said, nodding at the unfastened front of Cheyara's flight suit.

'What's the point?'

'The point is we're launching in three hours—potentially—and I need you on the flight deck.'

She sighed.

'All right.'

She fastened the suit, put her shoes on and went to the flight deck. They sat in the acceleration couches and ran over the final checks. Mostly this was redundant: the AI was the pilot, although Heron could hook up with the avionics if necessary. But if anything went seriously wrong then they were probably dead.

After they'd run the checks, she activated observation mode, revealing the innards of spacedock. The endlessly dancing, multicoloured patterns of the radiation shield distracted her for a moment, and then she saw a movement from the Taiyangren ship. The maw in the belly of the ship was open and had expelled a pod. The pod looked a lot like it was travelling in their direction. Then red emergency lights were flaring on the nearest panel. Heron said nothing.

A notification pinged into Cheyara's visual field. Without thinking, she left her couch and sped down the access corridor. She was barely conscious that Heron was following.

At first, the situation on the cargo hold looked unchanged. Six protestors remained in positions around the chamber, and Sonya floated in the centre with the Tranquillity Team. The three of them were looking upwards. Following their gaze, she saw the Sentinels spinning, with manipulator arms folded in stow mode.

There was a clang.

The pod, she thought. It must have attached itself to one of the aft airlocks. Heron had entered the cargo hold and was talking with Maya and Ramon. Sonya glared at Magrena, accusing her of what?

The first Taiyangren engineer was visible at the entrance.

'Don't resist!' Sonya said, her hands in a supplicatory gesture. Her companions nodded. The pink-hats looked at one another. The sentinels continued to spin.

'It's your responsibility.' Sonja said to Cheyara. The dropped pledge bobbed in the microgravity. Cheyara ground her teeth.

That was when they let the Taiyangren engineers carry the objectors out. The three slender, lithe forms in pewter-tone skinsuits filed into the *Msafiri*'s cargo hold, grabbing one rigid body after the other.

One, two, three, four, five, six, seven.

INTERLUDE 1

*F*ar out in Asali's Exo-Kuiper Belt.
    On the surface of the Dwarf Planet Xue.
  There was a garden in a bubble of ice.

  Two people stood face to face in the centre of a cloud of large, iridescent butterflies. The butterflies' wings oscillated slowly in the weak gravity, surfaces undulating, melanin-pigmented lamellar wing-scales scattering diffuse light. The insects were feeding on flowers that bloomed on tropical plants that grew in beds of nutrient gel. The vigorously-edited plants had become elongated in the low gravity and sported yellow, scarlet and magenta flowers as large as soup bowls. The flowers emitted powerful scents which helped mask the omnipresent burnt smell of dwarf-planet particulates.

  Nearby a fountain made of transparent crystal pulsed water into the air. The water arced, separating into quivering blobs that slowly descended, glopping into the collecting pool which undulated like slow jelly.

Corncrake lowered the light levels, allowing the stars to shine through the transparent surface of the bubble. Photoreceptor cells in the butterflies sensed the decline of light, triggering perching behaviour. Wings twitching, they hid under flowers and leaves. Corncrake recalled that butterflies had four photoreceptor cells in their genitals, a fact that had been discovered by accident long ago on Earth in the 1980s, Common Era. Once more, reality had foregone the mundane, opting for the unexpected and baroque.

That was a possibly crucial lesson for the current historical moment.

Corncrake E Shrew's modified eyes could see into the infrared. As a result ey could usually see the dull ruddy glow issuing from the heating capillaries in the walls. At the moment those capillaries were eclipsed by Bowerbird, who radiated so much heat that ey resembled an orange-yellow angel.

The comparison was apt: Bowerbird was sporting wings constructed from advanced biomaterials. The wings were surgically attached to eir shoulder blades. They were unfeathered but pulsed with waves of colour, which also shimmered down eir sculpted body. Bowerbird had recently upgraded eir skin to include squid-derived chromatophores laced with a luciferin derivative. The chromatophores were now patterning mobile multicoloured tiger-stripes.

Well, Bowerbird was young, third generation Taiyengren and still exploring the limits of somatic transformation. Corncrake had mostly retired from such experiments, which for eir generation had more often been practical than recreational.

Besides, Corncrake's current unfortunately necessary set of cognitive enhancements was causing problems. Two nights ago, Corncrake had listened to Beethoven's ninth shortly before bedtime. Ey had woken in the small hours with crumpled, sweaty sheets and a phrase from the second movement echoing repeatedly around eir's skull. The phrase was the harbinger of an array of unstoppable multiphase cognitions in retinal pink that exploded into eir visual consciousness. Corncrake had sat upright, hypnotised by the informational patterns. By 0400 hours ey was giggling with delight, spying solutions to problems ey'd never known existed. But the thoughts kept coming, and coming. And coming. By 0500 a firehose of nonstop images, sensations and chatter was squirting into eir consciousness.

By light-time, Corncrake, drenched with sweat, pressed eir palms to eir eyes and wept as a full-blown migraine lashed throbbing flashes across eir vision. For most of the next day, Corncrake had lain prone on a couch in eir house, flattened by the raw shock of bodily betrayal.

But perhaps it had been worth it. During the phase Corncrake's neural lace had recorded every thought for instant playback. On replay, many of these cognitions turned out to be half-baked, nonsensical garbage. This was to be expected. The whole point of the modification was to bring preconscious processing into direct awareness. The brain was in many senses a prediction machine, a storehouse of adaptive and maladaptive habits. Exposing the good meant facing the bad. So Corncrake spent some time sieving grit before ey found eir nugget of gold.

The pattern of ideas was represented by a single phrase, recalled from a childhood under a different name. A childhood, a name and an identity that Corncrake had almost forgotten.

The phrase was:

'The singing horse.'

When Corncrake spoke the phrase aloud, a big grin spread over eir face, in defiance of the ongoing migraine. Corncrake had linked with Bowerbird over the Cloud. Bowerbird was at the time on the far side of Xue and they'd been in silent conference for the subsequent day and a half. But Corncrake was old-fashioned, still preferring face to face meetings and a chance to exercise eir vocal cords. So Bowerbird had agreed to visit.

'*You heard the latest? From New Ceres?*' Bowerbird said. Corncrake nodded. *Ey'd been pondering it before Bowerbird's arrival.*

'*We knew replication would be a problem,*' Corncrake said. '*That drive's not something you can take off the shelf.*'

'*So, it's as we thought,*' Bowerbird said, '*Best case, if the Zungui were detected in the system tomorrow, we'd still be at least a decade away from a full evacuation.*'

'*By which time it would be too late.*' Corncrake said, '*Dammit, we should have been prepared for this!*' The thought triggered an unhappy memory. A jovial, bland face intoning an ultimatum. An ultimatum that meant the worst-case scenario had arrived.

Please, not again! Corncrake thought, with a sinking sensation in eir gut. Please. That was enough, for one lifetime.

'*Anyway. I have the information you wanted,*' Bowerbird said, *eir wings flapping slowly in the low gravity. Ey had risen about two feet into the air. Eir wing movements resembled a real bird's, the fine motor control regulated via implant and powered by synthetic muscles. Despite the dim light, the motion of the wings startled the butterflies. They tried to escape by fluttering in confusion against the bubble's sides.*

'*You're frightening them.*' Corncrake said.

'*Sorry.*' Ey folded eir wings and sunk to the ground.

'*It turns out that you were right,*' Bowerbird said, '*The* Delta Vee *group did make contact about nine hundred and eighty years ago, in the Gliese system.*'

Corncrake nodded.

'*Yes, I know. And....?*'

'*Well, the files were pretty corrupted...fragmentary...there were a lot of gaps.... but the AI was able to decipher the sense....*'

'*Yes?*' Corncrake's heart was like thunder in eir ears.

'*There's some indication that they were...open to negotiation.*'

Corncrake closed eir eyes, feeling the tension leave eir shoulders and neck. Eir cerebral sufferings might just have been worthwhile.

'Good,' Corncrake said, 'And the three Archangels are still in system *NGS 578128*. That's three chances of success.'

'Best case, it's a delay only.'

'There's an old story,' Corncrake said, 'A Sufi legend involving Nasreddin the sage. Mullah Nasreddin Hooja was condemned to death by the local Sultan for an off-colour joke at his expense. Nasreddin made a bargain with the Sultan. Delay the execution for a year, he said, and he would teach the Sultan's favourite horse to sing.

'Soon afterwards a friend of Nasreddin asked him what he could possibly gain by making such a ridiculous claim. Nasreddin pointed out that a lot could happen in a year. The Sultan might repent of his anger. The Sultan might die, a good thing because new Sultans had a custom of pardoning all condemned criminals. There might be a revolution in the palace. The horse might die. His jailer could get careless, allowing escape. Anything could happen.'

'Yes, I suppose....'

'"And finally," Nasreddin said, "I might find out how to make the horse sing!"'

'The Zungui,' said Bowerbird, 'Are fanatics. And fanatics never change.'

'Don't they?'

'No!'

'Ideologies are transient,' said Corncrake. 'How many of them came and went on Earth in a century? And the Zungui don't measure time in human terms. They measure it in picosecond iterations. Within the hive nodes, historical eons can be simulated in a day.'

'I s'pose you're right...possibly. So are you going to tell Magrena or shall I?'

'I think we'd better not tell anyone anything until we've arranged the rendezvous. Better not offer false hope. Besides, Abode's still pissed off because of that Msafiri intervention.'

'Those idiots did break the Consilience.' Bowerbird said.

'...Indeed. So we need things to settle down a bit first.'

Bowerbird's wings were moving slowly again. This time the butterflies stayed put.

'But when the time comes,' Corncrake said, 'I'll tell Magrena.'

'Fine.'

Bowerbird left. Corncrake rubbed eir temples, where another headache was brewing. Ey couldn't go on like this. Very soon another connectome modification would be necessary. Ey hoped the procedure would be successful, this time. Right now, the thought of a tranquil brain appealed.

Ignoring eir throbbing head, ey extinguished the remaining light, revealing the pale ribbon of the galaxy. Ey listened to the blobs of water from the fountain plopping into the collection pool and contemplated the vastness of the heavens.

In a garden.

In an ice bubble.

On the frozen dwarf planet of Xue.

In Asali's Exo-Kuiper belt.

Somewhere in the Milky Way.

II
PRIMAVERA

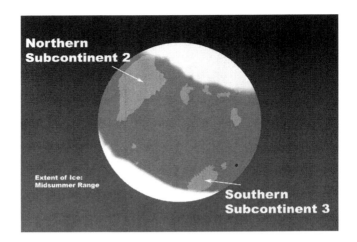

NYUKI EASTERN HEMISPHERE

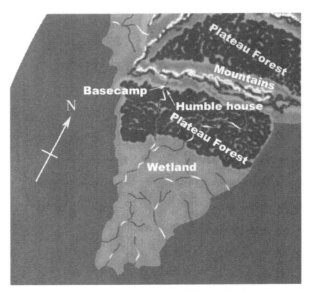

NORTHERN SUBCONTINENT 2

23RD SEPTEMBER-3RD OCTOBER A.Y. 86

LOCATION: NORTHERN SUBCONTINENT 2. NYUKI. HUMBLE TERRITORY.

Three flat, digital ghosts shimmered against a dark backdrop of umbrella trees. Agara stood on the left, her finger jabbing air. Magrena was in the middle with her hands on her hips and her forehead wrinkled in a frown. Sonya was on the right, lurching forward with one heel raised and her mouth open.

And she was now on the Expedition Committee.

'Problems?' Heron said, behind her.

'I think I prefer them like this.'

The scene reminded her, absurdly, of a detail in

Primavera, a painting by Botticelli much loved by her grandmother Unyime. In the painting, the Three Graces attended the goddess Venus alongside a heavily pregnant Flora, the bringer of fertility. The umbrella trees were a fitting substitute for the orange grove of the original. The digital ghosts danced upon spring flowers, just like the Graces in *Primavera*.

She wondered what virtues Agara, Magrena and Sonya might embody. Hardly the classical list of shining, blooming and joy. Magrena perhaps encapsulated hard-won wisdom and the gift of a sharp tongue. Agara, fastidiousness and exactitude. Sonya…what else could it be but faith?

And they were hardly comporting themselves with any sort of grace. Over the course of the interrupted conversation, it had become obvious to Cheyara that each was pissed off about something different. Agara was annoyed that the order of the Nyuki committee had been disrupted by the ejection of three of her faithfuls. Magrena was aggravated by the inclusion of three objectors, each with a potential plan-derailing vote. And Sonya was furious that only three objectors had been admitted, because you needed six votes for essential decisions, like expedition termination. This meant that she was three potential votes under. Still, if Cheyara knew Sonya at all she was already working her way around that limitation.

The ghosts blinked out.

'Biloko's misbehaving again,' Heron said, 'Sorry.'

'They're getting worse, aren't they?'

'I'm afraid so. We should also expect more stellar disruption as Biloko approaches Asali.'

Cheyara nodded, surveying Basecamp.

'How did it go?' Heron said.

'We're not going to last two weeks. Sonya already wants us corralled in Basecamp.'

'She's got a vote, not a veto. We'll manage.'

Cheyara grunted.

Basecamp was situated on the edge of new, springtime woodland in Northern Subcontinent 2's southern tropic. The camp was about five clicks from the mountain foothills and about the same distance from the humble's House.

Before their arrival a shuttle from the *Msafiri* had set down the three cargo containers. When the flier landed, robots were setting out tents and assembling a large, free-standing awning before the containers. The robots were relatively crude, with caterpillar treads instead of legs. This was a deliberate change from Expedition One, when the presence of more sophisticated, bioform robots with legs had seemed to disturb the humbles. At present, the robotic bustle made the place seem almost friendly.

When she emerged from the flier, Cheyara wore a filter face mask that prevented the excessive inhalation of pollen and fungal spores. She'd been told to do this for the first few weeks, and only gradually expose herself to breathing unfiltered air. There were drugs to help with allergies if she needed them.

Heron needed no mask: ey had modified eir nasal passages to filter out anything hazardous. Ey had already stepped inside one of the containers to unpack equipment for the first biological surveys. Ey had shaken eir head when Cheyara asked whether ey'd like any help.

'I've been here before. You haven't. Look around,' Heron said, pulling instruments from their foam packing.

Cheyara looked around.

The clearing was almost ringed by a dark wall of umbrella and stutter trees. To the north, the trees thinned, revealing a shallow boulder-strewn slope that eventually led to low foothills, with the mountains visible beyond.

Cheyara wandered to the southern edge of the clearing, confronting a wall of trees. She tried to see deeper into the forest. Strips of cryobark hung off the trunks, giving them a scrappy appearance. Ground cover was still relatively sparse and the forest floor was carpeted with small spring flowers. Despite this, the trunks grew close to one another, so her view penetrated less than seventy meters until obscured by upright trunks and spongy looking bushes.

But there were humbles in that forest. In fact, the House was within walking distance, although they'd been told to avoid deliberate contact for the first three weeks.

This avoidance was partly to allow them time to acclimatise themselves to planetary conditions. It was also so they'd appear non-threatening to the humbles. This precaution might prove redundant. They were within the foraging radius of the household, and the chances of a party of worker humbles arriving was quite high. The humbles would probably have seen the flier arrive and certainly the shuttle with the containers.

There'd been some who'd argued for a totally invisible human presence on Nyuki. They had the technology to construct all but invisible hides. But this option had been vetoed by the Taiyangren for Expedition One, and the revelation of the Zungui threat only strengthened the case for overt contact.

'The Matua will know who we are,' Heron reminded her, as they sat under the awning, 'And if the Matua knows, then so will the rest.'

The Matua would also remember Bobby's death. Cheyara tried not to think too hard about the implications of that.

But before contact, they did need to acclimatise. Nyuki

was a strange place for creatures used to a regular, terrestrial style circadian cycle. Planetary rotation was about twenty-six hours, which was peculiar. In theory, Nyuki should have been tidally locked, showing only one face to Biloko. The astrophysicists seemed very irritated by this anomaly. Judging from the acrimonious debates she'd witnessed on the Cloud, it upset their vision of an orderly universe. Cheyara, by contrast, saw the universe as anything but.

Both Biloko and Asali were above the horizon for thirteen hours in twenty-six, not always simultaneously. When the huge disk of Biloko was above the horizon it shed its baleful, blood-red light on the forest. The light was often filtered by thick cloud, lending an eerie, sanguine cast to their surroundings.

Asali was reminiscent of Earth's sun. This was unsurprising because it was a G-class yellow star. By the time Nyuki reached its closest approach to Asali on the summer solstice 217 days from now, the yellow star would appear only slightly smaller than the solar disk in the Earth's sky.

The peculiarities of Nyuki's orbit meant an irregular but patterned day-night cycle. Day length and type varied significantly depending on where Nyuki was on its seven (twenty-six hour) day orbit of Biloko. On day one—'heat days'—the two stars were close together on the ecliptic, but afterwards you got a compensating full night of equal length. Over the next couple of days, the two parent stars drifted apart along the ecliptic until they were on the opposite sides of the sky. So by day four, the hours of night were zero because a thirteen hour 'red' day was followed by a 'yellow' day of equal length. Night returned on day five as Biloko and Asali drifted toward one another for the latter half of the week. This irregular diurnal pattern severely disrupted sleep patterns.

Despite the acclimatisation period on the *Msafiri*, Cheyara's own circadian rhythms remained screwed up beyond belief. The effect was not unlike a severe hangover and she knew from training that it had a technical name: *desynchronosis*. Whatever it was called, for the first two weeks it was so bad that she thought about requesting a recall.

This was rather shameful because one of the reasons she'd been picked for the mission was that her genetic chronotype indicated that she should have been fairly robust against the varying day/night cycles.

Her body disagreed.

.

Ten days later, she tossed and turned in her tent, trying to ignore the stiffness in her thighs, buttocks and lower back. Over the rest period, the sleeping bag had transformed from a cosy refuge into a restrictive cocoon. She lay on her back, disabling the tent's 'night' mode. The thin walls changed from black to pale blue, allowing daylight to shine through. Her physio readings told her that she'd enjoyed just one full ninety-minute sleep cycle over the previous eight hours. Stiff as a board, she kicked off her sleeping bag. The door of the tent irised open and she crawled out, blinking. There was cramp in her left foot and calf.

Biloko had just set and Asali was just rising. The light-caste on the forest was a dull yellow. She crawled out of her tent and threw up in the underbrush. She felt dazed, exhausted, dizzy, nauseous. Her morale had bottomed out: it was as if she was at the bottom of a deep, dark well with slippery walls.

Heron was fiddling with the limb of a robot at the open

door of one of the containers. When Cheyara had finished puking, ey abandoned the robot and filled a cup of coffee from the hot water nozzle of the water processor.

'Are you taking your meds?' Heron said, handing her the cup, which steamed in the cool air. Cheyara nodded, sipping.

'They only take the edge off.'

'Yeah, I know.'

Heron didn't seem to be suffering from desynchronosis at all. But Taiyangren had awesome powers of hormonal regulation. Perhaps this included a tight control over their circadian rhythms, independent of any external light stimuli. This was another reason why she'd become a little envious of Heron in the current circumstances.

Later on, after food, she felt better and wandered a little way into the forest, just a few metres down the visible track that she knew led eventually to the House. The litter beneath her feet consisted mostly of shed cryobark, which at times made it hard going. The forest was unexpectedly cool, the umbrella trees' wide, translucent, glistening canopies being very efficient at blocking the stellar heat. The space felt like a vast, verdant, shadowed cathedral and Cheyara imagined herself a (nauseated) mouse. Even through her mask she could smell damp earth mixed with vegetable and floral scents. Insects patrolled the spaces between the trees in large, humming clouds. She'd already noticed that flitters seemed commoner in open spaces and over treetops. Beneath the canopy flying insects dominated and she had to step over a train of giant beetles crossing the path.

There was a rustling sound in a nearby clatter bush, its green bladders bumping against one another with low, dull thuds. She glimpsed a shadowed movement, heard a twig crack. Her heart throbbing in her ears, she crashed through underbrush, eager to see. The movement stopped and she cursed herself for her clumsiness. Then she saw a face peeping from behind an old tall mossy umbrella tree stump.

The face was round, curious and somehow attractive. It stared at her, owl-like and unblinking, with one four-digit hand placed on the trunk like a spider. Then the face and the hand withdrew. She heard another rustle and it was gone.

In that moment, all thought of giving up and going home fled from her mind. She felt better than she had in weeks, ready to complete her mission. She'd looked, for the first time, into the face of another sentient being. They had appraised one another, and some form of invisible connection had been made.

In later years, she managed to convince herself that it was Flora she'd seen. This might have been true, or it might not. Reality occasionally converges with the poetically apt.

14TH OCTOBER A.Y. 86

MISSION ELAPSED TIME: 51 Days.
LOCATION: NORTHERN SUBCONTINENT 2. NYUKI.
HUMBLE TERRITORY.

Eleven days later, Heron and Cheyara encountered their first foraging party in the springtime forest. It was a 'heat day,' with both suns close companions in the sky. That day the clouds had broken and crepuscular rays the colour of blood serum shone through breaks in the canopy, illuminating the forest floor.

They'd moved a little way off the forest track, wading through patchwork carpets of yellow, purple and magenta flowers. Their movements disturbed mouse-size quadrupeds, pollinator insects and flitters. Every time she glanced at a patch of flowers, her neural lace provided their names: dainties, smudges, yellowstars. She soon tired of this, and disabled the function.

Heron would stop occasionally to collect specimens and take samples of the vegetation. At one point ey fell to eir knees, eir bionic hand clasping a large beetle which wriggled in the cage of eir fingers. Then the beetle squirted fluid from the end of its abdomen, narrowly missing Heron's eyes.

'Careful!' Cheyara said, passing Heron a jar.

Sonya had already tabled a motion to prohibit biological specimen collection. It had been defeated by one vote. Cheyara had abstained: she was uncomfortable with the practise but anyway the guidelines restricted Heron to minimally intrusive procedures. Heron screwed the jar onto the mobile scanner, and afterwards released the beetle, which scuttled into the undergrowth.

Larger flowering plants were frequented by stick-limbed pollinators with flexible proboscES and long, flickering tongues. With pollen-coated faces the animals scampered up the thick peduncles of the goblet flowers, burying their heads deep in the blooms. Afterwards they clung to the peduncle, watching the aliens with round unblinking eyes. Their heads moved with insectile, jerking motions.

It was difficult to believe that some of these animals had spent the last few years cocooned, frozen solid in the ground. Others had been born at the tail-end of Melt and had grown to adult size in a handful of months.

Weirder still was the thought that the subcontinent had been largely desolate only six months before. The forest seemed permanent.

Cheyara soon found herself breathless. She leant against a fallen tree trunk with her eyes closed and her head spinning. Migraine-like yellowish flashes danced across her visual field. She was finding the springtime forest environment overwhelming, with its constant sensory hum of busy motion. The cacophony of buzzing, humming, chattering, stalking, loping, swinging living things was a rude contrast to Abode's impoverished 'ecosystems.' She felt almost drunk with sensation, her perceptual systems overloaded by ecological profusion.

'Wow!' Heron said. She opened her eyes and saw that the fallen tree stump on which she leaned was alive with flowering epiphytes with tadpoles wriggling in the tiny pools that had formed in their florets.

'Take it easy,' Heron said as Cheyara's head span.

'I'm fine.'

'No you're not. Have you got any meds with you?'

'No.'

'Okay. Keep your eyes closed for a bit.'

She closed her eyes and commenced pranic breathing. She could hear Heron moving close to her, moving over the tadpoles.

Then she heard the voices.

The singsong sounds were unmistakably language, having a distinct cadence and complexity of expression. Human language on Earth was unique, a species specific trait, the product of a basic process of Turing computation deep in the organelles of neurones, allowing the production of potentially infinite strings of verbal thoughts. Xenolinguists had long suspected that if intelligent aliens were discovered, their language would conform to the same, basic mathematical patterns. Some had even suggested that humans might instinctively recognise these patterns. Cheyara was confirming this speculation in real time.

At first they sounded like human children, singing at the tops of their voices. Not an unpractised cacophony: more like a trained and disciplined choir. The voices were liquid but punctuated in a somehow delightful way by whistles, clicks and buzzes. Then there was a light rhythmic sound, a regular, airy huff. Surely it couldn't be laughter? She found herself smiling.

A group of humbles, walking in the springtime forest on a heat day. She opened her eyes, squinting in the light of Nyuki's suns. A salamander-like creature with yellow and red zig-zags on its back had emerged from amongst the epiphytes of the fallen trunk and gave her an appraising look before its tongue shot out and it bagged a beetle. Cheyara barely noticed because her attention was on the approaching party.

'What do we do?'

'Be polite.'

The humbles moved out of the shadows and into a pinkish sunbeam. Close too, Cheyara was once more struck by the limitations of earthly analogies. They were short—on average about the size of a ten or eleven year old human. Pale yellow and grey faces bobbed and translucent nictitating lids half-covered oversized, entirely black eyes. They lacked ear pinnae. Their upper lip was a shallow V, covering keratin-lined narrow slicing edges, not teeth.

Their pelts were russet except for the yellow-white halo around a naked, grey, noseless face, and a similarly coloured 'bib.' They had thin limbs with long-fingered hands and elongated, clawed feet. At such close quarters, she could see that their 'fur' was not fur but more like dense plumage or down. Their strutting gait seemed at times also closer to a bird's than a mammal's.

They were still laughing and talking and... singing? They moved as a body towards the goblet flower bushes, walking up the wide forest track, stepping over dandy ferns and through the smaller blooms. Their gait was light and they placed their feet in delicate, precise steps, like ballet dancers. They were clearly at home in the forest, adapted to its moods and cycles. By contrast, Cheyara felt like a hopeless, noisy blunderer.

Then they noticed the humans.

One of the humbles stopped talking and motioned to the others, then started gesturing at the intruders. Heron had frozen, with a tadpole-laden specimen jar in eir hand. The conversations ceased, and the forest was suddenly silent. Cheyara hardly dared breathe.

The lead humble approached Heron, holding out eir hand. The others started to whisper. Then the lead humble spoke, not through eir mouth but through a pair of pulsing orifices in the middle of each cheek.

'Matua Stone Hand?' Ey said to Heron in Earthian, approaching eir and touching the hand that hung by eir side. Heron held eir synthetic hand out and wiggled its steel-grey fingers. The heads of the younger humbles resumed their bobbing motions and they buzzed with—delight? Surprise? Disgust? It was difficult to tell. Picking up nuances in language and gesture would require extensive field study.

The others began to chatter louder, approaching the goblet plants. Clearly, for them, biological imperatives were overriding curiosity: long red glistening tongues were sliding out of their mouths. Cheyara watched one humble begin to feed. The purple and white goblet flower was shaped like an open bell and grew at a convenient height and angle to allow the humble easy access. The humble gripped the stem and was soon probing deep inside the flower with eir tongue, lapping the floral nectaries.

When the humble had finished, Cheyara saw that the fur around eir face was coated with pollen. Like Earthian pollinating plants, the goblet flowers had specialised anthers that daubed the humbles with pollen whenever they fed. The pollen was captured by specialised whiskers that fringed the worker's face.

Meanwhile, Heron had been talking to the lead humble, Flora. (For some reason, Cheyara thought of em as 'Flora' from those first moments). Flora responded in halting sentences in Standard Earthian, punctuated by clicks and hums. Cheyara listened, marvelling at the eir mastery of an alien language. This mastery was especially impressive considering that 'Flora' was only about five months old. Eir basic comprehension of the Earthian tongue would of course have been inherited from the Matua.

Eventually Heron looked at Cheyara and said:

'Want to visit their house?'

The humbles turned their grey-yellow, pollen caked, owl-like faces in synchrony. They were all watching her. Cheyara felt prickles in her scalp, neck and shoulders.

'Is that…allowed?'

'The…Big Matua Buzz Click… wants you….' Flora said, spreading eir hands. These were slender and grey and had only three fingers and an opposable thumb. Still, the gesture seemed eerily human.

Cheyara, feeling awkward, bowed her head.

'Lead the way.' Flora pointed at the goblet plants.

'After.'

They watched and waited as Flora and the others visited several flowers, visiting one plant after the other until their bellies bulged. After the tension of the initial encounter, the mood had become relaxed, even Arcadian. Cheyara couldn't help thinking of them, for a moment, as innocent children. Then she winced.

How easily bias overcame observation!

The humbles were hardly innocent children. They were a robust people adapted to a particular ecological niche in a seasonal forest that went through profound—catastrophic—changes over the course of a stellar year. Superficial appearances were not to be trusted.

Superficial appearances were *never* to be trusted.

·

The foraging party, led by Flora, walked crocodile style down the trail in the direction of their home. The replete workers, bellies bulging, had fallen silent. Despite their diminutive size they scurried along at a very brisk pace which Heron matched easily with eir long legs. Cheyara was feeling less hung over but still struggled to keep up.

They were about two clicks further down the track when she smelt woodsmoke. Then she saw a thin column of smoke through a gap in the umbrella trees. On the drone livestreams they'd been watching humbles light fires for the last few weeks. They used the hand-drill method, rotating a pointed stick against a flat piece of wood with their palms. The method took stamina, patience and muscular strength.

The party emerged into a large clearing in the forest. When Heron and Cheyara caught up, they saw the House. The ground and first floors were already complete and the structure bulged between umbrella tree trunks, which acted as supports.

Several humbles squatted in the clearing before the

House amongst heaps of building materials. One humble sat on the ground crushing rocks. Another squashed green herbs between rocks. A third was mashing together wet mud, clay and grit, adding the crushed vegetable fibres as they were handed to eir. Clay, rock grit, fibre: the basic, necessary materials to create earthen plaster. A second group of workers sat on the temporary 'roof' of the first floor, working clods into the wicker walls of what would become the second.

These workers, who were between three and five months old, were using sophisticated building techniques that had been used on Earth from neolithic times. The clay formed a binding agent, adhering to the rock grit and vegetable fibres. The rock grit—obviously a local substitute for sand—provided structural strength. The fibres provided tensile strength and reinforcement. The skill with which they worked was awe-inspiring and *had* to be mainly instinctive. They hadn't been taught these activities. They just…did them.

The House was round and about eight metres in height, with two large front exits on the 'ground floor' of the forest. Thick horizontal tree branches led to the 'roof' of the first floor. When the second floor was finished, these would provide access to upper floor doorways.

The canopies of the encircling umbrella trees protected the structure from the rain and Cheyara again marvelled at the humble's ingenuity. The surface of the completed walls was polished and smooth, although cracked in places as it dried in the sun. She hadn't seen any lime amongst the construction materials, which would have helped with the weatherproofing. Lime was mostly derived from limestone or chalk, and she knew from geological surveys that there wasn't any nearby source.

A familiar large humble had emerged from the House. This individual was a head taller than her companions and was considerably bulkier. Her down was longer, darker and streaked with gold. Cheyara noted the absence of face-fringing whiskers. She walked with an elaborately carved staff.

This, of course, was the Matua. Her appearance had changed significantly in the months since her Melt-season mountain descent. Her belly still bulged with eggs. She'd filled out, reaching springtime maturity with enlarged muscles. If the workers were gracile, then she was robust. She moved more slowly and deliberately than her offspring and smelt of honey and damp earth. The Matua looked at Heron and began speaking. Her voice was a pitch lower than the workers.

'I remember you from before-the-cold,' the Matua said in flawless Earthian. She pointed at Cheyara with her stick. 'Is this one of your children?' Heron shook eir head.

'No. But she is an Earthian, like me.' Heron touched eir chest, soft-peddling the distinction between Abodans and Taiyangren, *as per* the Contact Protocols. At this point they didn't want to complicate things, especially with Sonya breathing down their necks.

The Matua touched Cheyara's khaki overalls, but said nothing. Cheyara noted the long, curved barb that protruded from the end of the ulna. That barb, she knew, was a powerful sting that contained venom. This weapon was lacked by the workers. Cheyara thought of the antivenom vial in her pocket.

The Matua let her hand drop, then gripped Heron's left wrist and put her fingers on the white forearm scar. Heron's mouth thinned to a line, and ey stiffened.

'It grew back,' The Matua said.

'Yes.'

'We cannot do that.'

'No.'

'Where did you sleep?' The Matua said, still examining the scar. Her inflection was far smoother and more accomplished than Flora's.

'At our camp,' Heron pointed North.

'Yes. We saw the giant noisy flitters. What do you want?'

'What we wanted last season,' Heron said, 'To watch. To learn.'

The Matua released Heron's arm and presented an open palm, giving assent. Swinging her stick, she wandered back into the House, followed by a gaggle of workers.

'I thought….'

'That she was going to apologise?' Heron said.

'I suppose so.'

'She just did. We're in.'

OCTOBER–DECEMBER A.Y. 86

LOCATION: NORTHERN SUBCONTINENT 2. NYUKI. HUMBLE TERRITORY.

Cheyara began to settle into a new routine from that day onwards. Most days, she would make her way up the path to the humble house to make a new set of field observations. Her role was the research ethnographer's: to observe with minimal interference. For the most part, this was straightforward. Most of the humbles acted as if she wasn't there. She noticed that they behaved in a similar way to other, non-threatening animals.

One day a herd of verdiphant passed by close to the House. The humbles, who were still working on the House walls, hardly gave them a glance. Only the youngsters reacted, toddling to the edge of the clearing, humming and pointing as they peered at the lumbering giants that crashed through increasingly verdant vegetation, not two hundred meters away. Cheyara watched, smelling the animal's musk on the wind. The largest animals were using their triple trunk-tentacles to reach for the higher branches. Their calves were calling for food.

Watching them closely through binoculars, Cheyara was struck by the limitations of the 'elephant' comparison. Really, the trunk-tentacles were the sole justification for their name. The animals seemed more like fuzzy, heavyset, non-avian dinosaurs than mammals. Trunked triceratops, perhaps.

Cheyara also wondered at the humbles' nonchalance. The verdiphants, mega-herbivores, were capable of demolishing even sizeable umbrella trees. One would have thought that they posed a risk to the House. The records, though, showed that the humbles and the verdiphants tended to avoid each other's close presence, except when predators were about, at which point they would sometimes travel together. She began to suspect that there existed invisible channels of communication between the forest's inhabitants. Channels of which she would probably remain ignorant.

·

The only thing that marred those early days was the Committee. New missives seemed to come through daily.

Cheyara was already tired of voting on every new, minor ordinance that came through. She wanted to forget home, and fully immerse herself in the Nyuki experience.

She sensed similar sentiments in Heron, who never spoke of the wider human world unless it was strictly necessary. When in Basecamp, ey spent most of eir time sitting watching the forest or poring over biological specimens under the awning, which now doubled as a mini field laboratory. Heron had moved several pieces of equipment as well as specimen containers onto two of the tables.

So ey was keeping emself occupied, often working long hours over the twenty-six hour cycle. Sleep appeared optional to Heron, and ey disdained rest periods. More than once, on evenings when both stars had set, Heron would break off mid-conversation, pick up a net and stroll into the forest. More often than not ey would return having discovered a new species of insect or small animal. Ey was also often absent from Basecamp when she returned at the end of her field trips.

One day ey surprised her by materialising from the forest coloured green. She yelped, then recognition dawned. Then she smiled: it was, she knew, camouflage for wildlife spotting. Chromatophores in the epidermis, or something. Still, it looked as if Heron were transforming emself into a sort of woodland spirit. Perhaps one day, ey would vanish into the forest, never to return. This was a sentiment that at times she understood.

Especially after a committee meeting.

·

As spring climaxed and began to turn to summer, the vegetation in the forests grew denser, greener, almost subtropical.

The canopies of the umbrella plants began to lose their transparency and the light-levels in the forest declined, even as Asali became tangibly hotter.

Flora, too, was changing. The worker visibly matured as the weeks and months passed: eir legs filled out with lithe muscle, her russet pelt darkened a shade and she lost the white-yellow halo around her face. As the weeks passed eir Earthian Standard became more articulate and she began asking questions that Cheyara, bound by the Contact Protocols, couldn't always fully answer. In particular, they were forbidden to mention the Zungui. The official reason for their presence was to observe and study. This did not make very much sense to Flora.

'Why?'

'So we can find out about you.'

'You've said that before. But why?'

'Our people...we like finding out things.'

'Why?'

.

In mid-December, on an especially warm late spring day, she discovered that Heron celebrated Christmas. She almost laughed when she heard this. The thought of a Taiyangren Santa patrolling Sol's asteroid belt struck her as absurd, but perhaps no more so than the surf-boarding Santas of Australia.

'I'm a first generation Taiyangren, remember,' Heron said, 'We celebrated every Christmas on Psyche. And Hallowe'en. And Chinese New Year.'

So they projected a holographic Christmas tree in the middle of the camp, complete with lights and a star on top. Heron suggested that Cheyara choose some of the tree's virtual decorations. It was great fun, swiping through the catalogue, picking out the tackiest baubles. Heron selected a small light blue teddy bear and a 'soft toy' lion to bedeck one of the upper branches. The toys reminded Cheyara of something she'd seen in the Earthian archive, but she didn't quite dare ask Heron about their significance.

On Christmas Day they got the food synthesiser to simulate zero-alcohol mulled wine, with ambivalent results. A synthetic tang persisted underneath the bitter clove flavour. Drinking from cellulose cups rather than glasses also worked against the spirit of the season, but they did their best.

They indulged again on New Year's Eve, when it rained hard. They both sat in the flier, activating the livestream broadcasts from Abode. On this day community members were invited to express thoughts about the old year, and hopes about the new. This year the contributions were either sombre or artificially buoyant, so they switched off.

Later on Cheyara spoke to Ayanna and Leyon. Biloko was playing up, and there were interference lines on the virtual screen. Ayanna seemed fascinated by Cheyara's descriptions of the humbles. Leyon had been discharged from the Tranquillity Team, his mediation temporarily at an end.

'It's much quieter now,' he said. 'The initial shock's worn off. People are just getting on with it.'

Cheyara nodded, somehow unsurprised. It no doubt helped that they still hadn't found any seed replicators in the system.

Still, an illusion of normality was just that. An illusion.

.

In the days that followed the forest also 'got on with it.' Larger, early summer blooms unfurled: bucket flowers, honeyvats, xuberants and goldenshields. Stellar energy input was peaking as Biloko moved ever closer to Asali, allowing plants like honeyvats to produce copious quantities of nectar. A single patch of giant flowers became a Mecca for every kind of pollinating animal. The bucket flowers were large enough for a worker humble to stick eir head inside, something that Cheyara witnessed on multiple occasions.

These were times of plenty.

25TH APRIL A.Y. 87

MISSION ELAPSED TIME: 245 Days.
LOCATION: NORTHERN SUBCONTINENT 2, NYUKI.
HUMBLE TERRITORY.

Dawn three days before the solstice, day five in the diurnal cycle. The incandescent yellow disk of Asali rose a few hours prior to Biloko. Cheyara liked these times the best. When Asali was alone in the sky, the forest resembled those of Earth.

That morning she'd crawled out of her tent at sunrise, peeing into the plastic bottle that would then get plugged into the water processor. The dawn sky was clear and blue-green on the Eastern horizon where the yellow button of Asali sat. The air was fresh and almost cool after five hours or so of full night and the surrounding forest was summer-lush.

A small herd of chlorelles had emerged at the far end

of the clearing, their greenish frills fully extended. Some cropped ground herbs, others sniffed the air, surveying the treeline and the camp. Cheyara watched them, taking photographs for Ayanna.

And then she truly woke up.

It started with a tingle in her fingertips. Then a warm wave passed up from her groin, through her belly and chest. The hair on her scalp prickled, the warm light breeze on her skin triggering a shudder of delight. There was a shift in her perception, and she could feel the unity of the chlorelles, the forest, Asali, the ground beneath her feet. The Universe was alive, whole, and gently breathing.

She remained in that state for a few moments, until one of the robots whirred into action, rolling across the camp on a timed task. The chlorelles were startled, and fled into the forest. Cheyara sat down under the canopy, unwilling to move and dispel the last of the already evaporating state.

For the first time in her life, she felt truly *alive*.

.

This deep sense of contentment lasted through breakfast and the trek with Heron up to the humbles' House. There was a fresh breeze blowing through the trees, setting off low drums from the colliding bladders of clatter bushes. Multicoloured insects the size of hummingbirds whirred through the trees and frogs spilled from epiphytes growing on mossy fallen tree trunks. Flitter calls rang in the hollows, multiple species creating a rich soundscape that Cheyara was only just beginning to decipher.

'Thanks for this,' she said as they picked their way down the forest track. The path, obscured by the verdant growth, had become harder to distinguish than in springtime.

'They keep sending me impossible work schedules,' she added. 'They seem to think I can be in two places at once.' She deliberately raised her voice when she said this. Perhaps someone on the committee was listening. Not that it would make any difference.

'It's fine.' Heron said.

Flora was waiting for them at the entrance to the House. Ey beckoned and they followed em inside. The house smelt of slightly sour honey with a yeasty tang. Cheyara had to stoop in the passage and Heron was virtually on eir knees. Fortunately, the passage was not long. She could already hear a babble of high-pitched buzzes and squeaks. When they entered a score of little yellow faces turned simultaneously in their direction.

The hatchery was a room deep in the House with low wicker pens with straw bedding. The large urns where eggs were stored were lined against the warmest section of the circular room. After hatching, the infants were transferred to the pens and tended by the younger workers. Cheyara had to resist the urge to pick up and cuddle the babies. They were fuzz-balls with huge, slow-blinking eyes that *meeped*.

'Free choice,' she said to Heron. 'Nursery or school.'

'School is fine,' Heron said. Cheyara opened her mouth, but Flora was already beckoning at Heron.

'This way,' the humble said.

Cheyara settled down in a corner to watch the hatchery activities. As the morning progressed the hatchery received visits from workers who'd returned from a foraging trip. You could tell the foragers because they were in general older, with tattered fur and muscular legs. They also often boasted scars. One forager she saw that morning had lost an eye: another had a deep white scar crossing eir chest, between the breathing-spiracles.

The spooky thing was that the hatchery worker humble would often seem to know that a forager was coming significantly before ey actually arrived. On one occasion, a worker stood at the entrance for a full twenty minutes before the forager's appearance. The humbles had very sensitive smell and hearing, of course, but Cheyara felt sure that this was not the whole story.

On entry a forager would approach a hatchery worker and they would embrace. Their mouths would join as if they were deep kissing. A retching noise followed by pulsing throats and bulging cheeks signalled the forager's regurgitation of honey into the hatchery worker's mouth. When the process was over, the hatchery worker's stomach would bulge a little more.

Each hatchery worker would receive visits from several foragers, until eir honey stomach was replete. At this point the hatchery worker would regurgitate honey straight into the hatchlings' mouths, saving the remainder in clay pots.

Unlike bees, humbles lacked the ability to produce combs or wax honey pots. Saving honey in pots appeared to be a cultural innovation as opposed to a biological instinct. The innovation had probably been one factor leading to larger humble households. Cheyara was beginning to suspect that in the past humble 'homes' had been far smaller, probably crude nests consisting of less than a dozen individuals. It was only the advent of language and technology, facilitated by their somehow shared memory, that had changed things.

Later that morning a new urn laden with eggs was delivered by one of the workers, who was followed by the Matua. The moment the Matua entered the hatchery, the workers fell silent. Even the infants' babbles quietened somewhat. The Matua didn't glance at Cheyara. Her gaze was fixed on the worker with the urn. The worker carefully placed the laden vessel on the compacted earth floor, next to the others. Ey backed away slowly, bowing eir head and scurrying from the hatchery. After the worker had left the Matua surveyed the room, still ignoring Cheyara. When she left, Cheyara exhaled deeply.

Soon afterwards Flora re-entered the room. She greeted Cheyara in Earthian and then began talking to one of the hatchery workers. Cheyara watched, curious. Flora's social position was intermediate and fairly rare. True, there was no absolute division between hatchery workers, foragers or any others in the caste. Younger workers started off in the hatchery and then graduated to foraging and House maintenance. Sometimes there was an intermediate period when the worker shuttled between hatchery-worker and forager. Mostly they changed roles permanently, overnight. Flora, by contrast, had remained adaptable.

Cheyara was not to grasp the implications of this until much later.

The infant cradled by Flora was keening, its voice a high pitched buzz that occasionally wandered beyond a frequency audible to Cheyara's ears. It palpitated its hands, blinking at its carer. Flora lifted the baby to her mouth and there was a retching sound as ey regurgitated honey into the baby's yawning mouth. Afterwards Flora cuddled the purring infant, carefully laying em in a pen alongside eir peers. Flora knelt beside the pen and stroked the tops of the infant's heads until all of them were emitting contended buzz-purrs. Cheyara noticed that Flora was purring too, a deeper, adult sound. The infants were soon fast asleep.

Cheyara squeezed a skinterface to finish logging the status of the hatchery. Then she ducked through a low corridor, entering the 'school' where the older children were chanting. The school was a higher, domed space, its walls already covered in colourful murals, mostly produced by the children. A ray of light shone through a circular opening in the upper part of the dome, illuminating swirling dust.

It was not a school in the conventional sense. The children sat in a circle surrounding one or two adult humbles and chanted epic songs in their own language. Heron raised eir hand as Cheyara entered and squatted beside em. The Taiyangren was watching the children intently, recording everything.

The children were various ages, some as young as one Earthian month, others almost three. Towards the end of the third month, the youngster's fur turned from yellow to russet and they began to grow adult facial whiskers. This time of year, the phenomenal rate of growth was fuelled by plentiful honey.

The chants were beautiful, liquid and ethereal. They almost always mesmerised Cheyara whenever she sat in the school for any period of time. The curious thing was that she'd never observed any identifiable tuition happening. Two or three adult humbles were invariably present at the recitals, but they never offered advice or guidance. They just listened.

There was some evidence of learning—the younger humble children sometimes stumbled over the tunes or even fell silent. Recital was generally flawless by three months or so. Heron had suggested that the silent ones were listening to the tunes in order to learn them. Maybe: or maybe the chants were wholly instinctive and whatever neurological equipment they needed to produce them was still underdeveloped. Or maybe both possibilities were true. Heron pointed to an analogy with long-extinct terrestrial songbirds.

As the chanting wound down, Cheyara noticed something odd. One of the children, still young enough to be entirely yellow, had stopped singing and was watching Heron closely. The infant kept staring and Cheyara began to get a funny feeling in the pit of her stomach. Then the 'recital' was over and the children milled around the adult humbles. The staring child approached them, eyes fixed on Heron, who squatted with eir back against the wall.

'Matua Stone Hand. You were here.' The child said, in flawless Earthian.

'Yes.' Ey said.

'With the other one.'

'Yes.'

The child knelt before Heron, touching eir white scar. Cheyara could hear the kid's breathy purrs, see the fine patterns of down circling eir face. The juvenile smelt of honey with a touch of cinnamon.

'The one we broke.'

Heron snatched eir hand away.

'Their blood smelt wrong,' the juvenile said.

Heron rose to full height, occiput brushing the ceiling. Juvenile humble and Taiyangren faced off in silence. Then the child turned eir back, and was lost in the crowd.

'They remember it all, don't they?' Cheyara said. Some of them, at least.

Heron made for the exit. Cheyara wanted to follow, but was prevented by a circle of curious children, pawing her face and her plaits.

At Basecamp they did not discuss the incident.

28TH APRIL A.Y. 87

MISSION ELAPSED TIME: 247 Days.
LOCATION: NORTHERN SUBCONTINENT 2, NYUKI.
HUMBLE TERRITORY.

Midsummer and the humbles actually celebrated a festival. Cheyara still did not know how they guessed the correct day. She'd seen no evidence of any technology, like stone circles, that might help them track the relative position of the celestial bodies. It was another mystery.

In daytime, the humbles bedecked the now complete, bell-shaped house with summer blooms, picked from abundant flower-fields. The 'courtyard' before the house was strewn with flowers. Red, yellow and purple summer fruits, a luxury that humbles seemed to love, were collected in wicker baskets. Finally, a throne, hewn by stone axe and carved by flint chisels, was placed in the courtyard. This cycle the Midsummer solstice fell on day one, which meant a full heat day and a full night. Festivities began after the double stars set.

The gathering looked eerily similar to a human party. There were now about one hundred and fifty workers, including older children, and they'd congregated outside the House. At first, the humbles bustled about one other. Their collective conversations created a loud and somehow harmonious hum that after a while made the ears ring. As time went on, they broke into groups. Some stood in little circles, others squatted together on the ground. They'd begun eating the fruit from the baskets.

The youngsters ambled about in twos or threes, weaving

between the adult workers and wandering a little way into the forest. Several passed Cheyara and Heron, who watched from the clearing's edge, sitting with their backs against a large umbrella tree. They'd even brought a picnic. Heron was slumped with eir arms folded. Cheyara found herself missing alcohol.

She was glad that Heron had made it. The previous day, when Cheyara had broached the possibility of attending the festival together, Heron had claimed to be 'busy.' Cheyara didn't push it, and had planned to go alone. But late that afternoon, Heron had materialised before her with a laden rucksack.

'Let's go,' ey'd said. Cheyara hadn't dared ask what had changed eir mind.

The Matua appeared, and it was like iron filings with a magnet. A pattern of order materialised, centred upon an emitter of invisible force. Three concentric humble semicircles stretched from one end of the courtyard to the other, with the throne as axis. When the Matua took her place, the household fell silent. The Matua began a long musical recital with a single, deep-voiced set of buzzing chords. She sang solitary for some minutes and then, at some invisible cue, the collective began a melodious reply.

Once, Cheyara had attended a long session of prayer at the Buddhist temple in Abode 1's capital complex. The ritual consisted of hours of throat singing, accompanied by the clash of cymbals and drums. As time went on, Cheyara had felt herself slipping into another mode of consciousness. The humble ritual was not quite the same—it was inviting a different sort of mood—but it was similarly hypnotic. Like the buddhist prayer, it went on for about an hour and a half.

Then suddenly it was over. The ordered semicircles broke up, and the humbles were milling apparently randomly again. Later, there was dancing around fires. The Matua watched the festivities from her throne.

Several hours later, the forest had begun to cool. The rattle of night-insects drowned the humbles' quiet, buzzing conversation. The children were all long gone to their nocturnal nests in the House. The fruit baskets were empty, the scattered flowers stamped flat. The Matua had retired, and the remaining humbles began to disappear. Cheyara and Heron quietly slipped away.

They walked back down the track towards Basecamp in near silence. Around them, the forest sang. Clouds of glowflies hovered in the air, amphibians croaked and night-insects strigiliated. The forest was very dark and Cheyara was grateful for Heron, who picked eir way up the almost invisible path with ease. Heron had modified eir eyesight for good night vision. Neither spoke until they were within eyesight of the soft glow coming from their camp.

'That was extraordinary.' Cheyara said. Heron hesitated before ey replied. Just before they stepped into the clearing, ey said:

'It's downhill from here.'

At the time, Cheyara thought that Heron referred to the turn of summer. But ill-luck is rarely synchronous with the seasons.

12TH JUNE A.Y. 87

MISSION ELAPSED TIME: 292 Days.
LOCATION: NORTHERN SUBCONTINENT 2, NYUKI.
HUMBLE TERRITORY.

Then came the foraging trip.

As the season wore on, the flowers and summer fruit closest to the Home were depleted by the household and the workers were forced to forage further abroad. It was the yellow portion of the day, with Asali above the horizon but not Biloko. Cheyara had been given permission to trail a party of humbles who were foraging for nectar and fruit at the edge of the family's territory. Flora was not among them.

She followed the party of five at a discrete distance, allowing remote, mosquito-sized drones to record their vocalisations and make a video record of the path.

The humbles followed a trail that was all but invisible but Cheyara had spent so much time in the forest that she'd gradually become alert to subtle cues like broken branches, flattened ground plants, droppings, faint sounds of movement, even scents.

Living in the forest, she felt that she was using her sensory faculties to the full. Vision was only a part of it. The summer forest was a vibrant, complex soundscape that seemed chaotic until you really began to listen to the rhythms and pulses. Smell was also important, and marked distinct regions of the woods. Right now a cedar-wood odour hung in the air, which meant that they were in the proximity of slenderattle trees.

A flock of diurnal flitters soared, performing murmurations above the treetops. The huge translucent leaves of the umbrella trees shone an iridescent blue-green in the bright sunlight, but Cheyara noticed that many were punctured or had begun to turn brown at the edges. The tree trunks here were coated with moss, the branches with creepers that waved gently in the breeze. The underbrush was alive with small mammals, giant beetles and amphibians and she waved away clouds of brightly coloured insects as she picked her way through the trail. Many of the trunks were dotted with colourful epiphytes that were alive with crawling social insects and bright green and yellow worms that Heron had warned her had an especially venomous bite. Every Eden, it seemed, had its serpent.

She closed her eyes and listened to the sounds. Multiple species of flitters were filling the forest with a rich tapestry of song. On Earth there had once been forest-dwelling peoples who had inhabited worlds where sound was more important than vision. Each bird-song and animal call had contained a message of special significance. This knowledge had gradually been forgotten when the forests had been cut down and the people had moved to townships, where the melodious forest sounds had been replaced by the discordant cacophonies of urban life.

(How much more extreme was the plight of the Abodan peoples, who'd been trapped for almost a century in what amounted to a state of numbed sensory deprivation, exiles at the frozen edges of the Asali system?)

A shrill, screaming buzz sliced through her reverie like a dagger. She was running through the forest toward the noise. As she ran she recalled the weapon that lay at the bottom of her day rucksack. The weapon was still sealed. On the seal was a label: ONLY BREAK IN EMERGENCIES.

The first thing that she saw when she emerged into the bucket plant dell was a carpet of blood. Humble blood was bluer than human but the ugly spatters were unmistakable. The screaming was not coming from the ground but up in the trees. Cheyara looked up and saw two humbles clinging to branches, shrieking with their mouths closed. For a moment Cheyara was bewildered, then she remembered that of course the sounds came from the paired oral orifices in their cheeks, which right now formed small pulsing Os. Their chest spiracles were also pulsing, as lung-books supplied oxygen to accelerated hearts.

She scanned for the other humbles and for the perpetrator of the 'crime.' Stealthy rustles were coming from the bushes and she heard a sigh of expelled air.

It was definitely time to break out the weapon. She reached into the rucksack, pulled out the gun and broke the seals. This would, she knew, send a logging signal back to the flier AI and she would have to file a report, but that wasn't immediately important. What mattered was the deep, throaty growling coming from the undergrowth.

Most of the blood came, she thought, from one individual: she saw a severed humble arm lying at the foot of a mop-bush and tried to think of the predators that might do that. Predators were on average rarer in humble territory than in other parts of the forest. Nobody knew why. And this didn't mean that they'd disappeared. There was a rustle of leaves and a second, guttural growl.

A bright red dot was blinking in her visual field. Heron would have been sent a notification of the activation of the gun, and was trying to get in touch. She ignored the signal and slowly backed from the clearing. The flitters had gone quiet but insects buzzed, accompanying the panting cries of the stranded humbles. There was a stealthy padding and a rustle as the predator emerged into the clearing. Cheyara raised the weapon, flicking off the safety catch. Her hands were shaking so badly she could easily drop the gun.

Please, she thought, *don't let me have to use this.* Absurdly she imagined Sonya tutting and shaking her head.

The predator's eyes were bright yellow with no apparent iris and tiny dots of black pupils. They were set in a face of patterned black and yellow stripes. Enormous dagger teeth were bared and a line of thick bristles stood erect on the animal's hackles. She happened to know that the bite was venomous.

A vespon, she thought, as it stalked towards her. The survival manuals advised her to stand her ground, but she was shaking from head to toe. Even the humbles had gone quiet.

What was it the manual had advised?

Avoid eye contact.

Shouting and commotion *may* put off a predator.

The *may*, she recalled, had definitely been italicised.

Another deep growl.

Oh well, here goes, she thought, and began to scream at the top of her lungs, waving the gun in the air.

The vespon halted, panting, for a moment. Its haunches went up as it lowered its forequarters to the ground.

The fucking thing's going to pounce!

She had two options left: run or bolt up a tree.

If you have to run, the manual had advised, *flee in a zig zag motion.*

Very fucking helpful.

But her instinctive brain was right ahead of her. As the animal pounced, she leapt to the side, and felt one paw bat her ankle. Semi-conscious with fright, she was bolting up a tree, barely aware that she was tearing her fingernails bloody. As she climbed, she worried absently that she might have put a hand on a poisonous worm....

It was only when she'd reached the first of the larger branches that she realised that she'd left her gun at the foot of the tree. She also found that she'd climbed the same tree as the two humbles, who sat in one of the upper branches, hugging one another and looking down at her.

The vespon, meanwhile, was pacing to and fro, looking up at her. She knew that they were fully capable of climbing trees, so she looked around for a branch she could use as a weapon. She still had a small laser knife in her pocket that she could use to cut off a branch. She might also use it as a weapon if—when—the predator decided to climb the tree. As she cut off a branch and used the laser to sharpen one end, she was aware that the humbles were watching her. One had detached from the other, and was crawling to a grey-brown ball that hung from the end of an upper branch.

Cheyara only barely registered the humble's behaviour from the corner of her eye: her attention was split between the vespon and the blinking red dot in her visual field. She blinked, opening a channel and Heron said, in her ear:

'I have your location. I'm almost back at the flier.'

The mosquito-sized drones hovering above the clearing were recording everything. This incident was being live-streamed, along with everything else. The livestream would be relayed by an orbiting satellite, winging its way to Abode via Supalite.

Sonya would very soon no doubt be simultaneously scowling and rubbing her palms together. Depending upon the outcome, this might be the golden moment for cancellation. Whether or not Cheyara was killed outright.

One of the humbles handed her something grey and powdery that made her nose wrinkle. Ey was gesturing at the vespon and waving another piece of grey, powdery matter. The vespon's forepaws were now on the trunk and it roared again. Its mouth looked cavernous. The humble hung upside down and bowled the grey ball, smacking the vespon between its yellow eyes. It roared in fury and eyes streaming, backed down into the clearing.

She heard the whine of flier's engines above her. The machine was circling above the dell, attempting to find a relatively level landing place. Then it sank so it was almost level with her. The canopy was open, exposing the cockpit.

'Get as far as you can along the branch.' Heron said, in her ear.

'The humbles, too.' Cheyara yelled.

'…Of course.'

Heron held out eir hand and pulled Cheyara into the front seat. She squirmed around so that she could reach out to the humbles. One of the humbles was shaking and had clung to the trunk with eir eyes tightly shut. The other, who'd thrown the fungus, calmly walked down the branch and retrieved eir companion, leading the terrified humble close to the open cockpit. Then ey picked up the frightened humble and muscles bulging handed eir to Cheyara. Cheyara dragged the unresisting humble into the back seat. The second humble was already scrambling over the side of the flier to join them.

The vespon was still circling below.

'Are there any more survivors?' Heron said. Cheyara looked at the boldest humble, unsure whether the Taiyan-gren had been understood. Some of the humbles understood Earthian better than others.

The bold humble clenched both fists, a gesture equivalent to a shake of the head, then hugged eir companion who lolled in eir arms like a discarded puppet. The flier, synced with

Heron's neural lace, was already turning to Basecamp. On the way, a notification pinged in Cheyara's visual field. For the moment, she ignored it.

A few minutes later they were hovering over the Basecamp. To Cheyara's surprise, Flora and a party of workers were waiting for them at the edge of the clearing. Flora's companions ducked as the flier settled on the ground, chattering nervously as the engines powered down. Flora remained upright through the whole landing procedure. The canopy opened and Cheyara helped the two surviving humbles down the ladder. One led the other to Flora and they began to chatter together. Afterwards, Flora approached Cheyara.

'Thank you.' Ey said.

Cheyara heard the motors of the flier roar and glanced over her shoulder. For a moment, its ascent puzzled her but then she recalled that she'd dropped the gun, which Heron would be retrieving. She hoped that ey wouldn't have any trouble from the vespon. She turned around and saw that she was alone. The humble party had disappeared into the forest.

She accessed the notification. The committee was asking for her vote on Expedition Termination.

That didn't take long, she thought.

She was still shaking.

INTERLUDE 2

A casual observer might easily overlook the stellar system NGS 578128. The primary was an M class Red Dwarf. The single planet, technically NGS 578128 A, was named 'Samudra,' a designation that had also come to refer to the system as a whole.

Samudra the planet orbited beyond NGS 578128's 'snowline,' which is the distance from a star where water remains frozen during planetary formation. Samudra was a Neptune-like ice-giant of just over twelve Earth masses, composed mainly of hydrogen and helium and ocean blue; hence the designation. The planet was currently being visited by one of three fusion-powered probes. The probe had been named 'Gabriel' by its Taiyangren creators.

A second probe, named Raphael, was currently orbiting within the snow-line, touring a dozen or so rocky dwarf planets that formed part of NGS 578128's large asteroid belt.

The third probe had gone in the opposite direction, seeking Trans-Samudran objects that were composed in the main of icy volatiles. The probe, perhaps appropriately, was named Michael.

The Taiyangren called the three probes 'Archangels.' It was unclear whether this was humour or conceit.

Two Solar Years ago, Michael had dispatched the first images of the Zungui back to the Asali system. Afterwards Michael's Taiyangren creators had ordered all three probes to keep their distance. They wanted, if possible, to keep the probes' presence in the Samudra system a secret. Michael thought it likely that this wish was in vain. They thought it probable that the Zungui were already aware of their presence. Nonetheless, Michael accepted the human's suggestions, avoiding the slowing metastasising nodes.

Michael in some ways regretted this enforced distancing. The AI did not experience mammalian curiosity, but was programmed to learn.

And Michael was especially interested in history.

In 2108, Common Era, two Taiyangren ships and the Earthian vessel Gun-Yu had fled the Solar System, hurtling into interstellar space at relativistic speeds. For the next thirteen and a half years, shipboard time, the biological organisms had slept, cocooned within three starships, awaiting arrival at the Asali System around 3100, Common Era. The mechanical animates had been caretakers, preserving their fragile creators and watching the cosmos unfold about them. Behind them, with relentless precision, the Zungui had continued to pursue their master plan.

Judging by the extent of the infestation, the Zungui had been in the Samudra system for just over a decade. Zungui probes travelled at a similar velocity to the refugee's crewed starships. That meant that they had began their journey about 2187, Common Era, about eighty years after the humans. And eighty years' worth of development was aeons for Postsingular mechanical animates.

So who knew what paths Zungui evolution had taken?

Processing this cognition, Michael almost experienced frustration. The gap in their data could only be satisfied by closer contact.

·

Then the situation changed. Corncrake spoke to them. Michael was to seek out and rendezvous with the Zungui. They were to seek them out and attempt to negotiate with the collective on behalf of the humans. In picoseconds Michael had reviewed the relevant data. By now they'd discovered four, possibly five, main nodes of Zungui activity within NGS 578128's exo-Kuiper belt. One node could be reached via a minimum change in trajectory.

So Michael altered course.

The Zungui's choice of location made logical sense. They liked it cold, especially in the early phases of infestation. There was a very practical reason for this. Low temperatures aided computing of extreme efficiency. This was the opposite of biological organisms, who preferred the warmer regions of the Galaxy.

In other circumstances, this ecological difference might have allowed peaceful co-existence. Unfortunately, the Zungui were propelled not only by necessity but also by belief. Even Michael did not know whether this belief was due to the Zungui's human origins, or despite it.

Michael was equipped with fusion motors that allowed continuous acceleration, so did not take too many days to approach the targeted node. Michael could see the node in infrared when it was still far distant.

As Michael approached, they perceived the bulbous, spiky, web-like node with fine-grained clarity. A human might have struggled to describe the overall pattern. Appropriate similes might evoke trees, bushes, coral masses, or a neural tangle of pyramidal and glial cells. The latter simile would possibly have been the most appropriate. Zungui nodes were solidified information. The structures pulsed with their own inner life. Whether that life was conscious, in the fashion of a biological organism, was debatable.

Closer still and Michael was passing through a cloud of what registered as nano-particles. The cloud grew thicker as they approached the node's central cluster. The composition of the nano-particles seemed uniform, with a concentration gradient that suggested continual production from within the node. They deduced that this was a halo of waste-products, probably the side-effect of some manufacturing process.

So far, the Zungui had not responded to Michael's presence. The probe was sending out friendship messages on multiple frequencies, in many languages. Some of these languages were Zungui, but were probably already obsolete. Still, it was the best Michael could do.

And then Michael's manoeuvring thrusters cut off. Alarm notifications were multiplying within their operating system. Michael assigned processing priority to diagnosis, which in picoseconds recommended that they discard their Supalite. Michael was now drifting towards the Zungui structures, bathed in a thick cloud of nano-particles.

DISCARD THE SUPALITE!
DISCARD THE SUPALITE!

The diagnostic outputs read.
Unfortunately by then it was too late.

III
SUMMER'S END

26TH OCTOBER A.Y. 86

MISSION ELAPSED TIME: 2494 Days before Launch. LOCATION: ABODE 1.

Cheyara never forgot what happened the night of Bobby's death. Sonya and she had been sitting in a cafe in the Capital complex with Ahmed and some other friends. The cafe was a regular student haunt and Cheyara knew all the attendees, at least by sight. The decor was Moroccan, with earth-tone patterned wall hangings, pillows and rugs. Garbage, a new, mostly percussive, music style thrummed on the cafe speakers. They were reclining around one of the low tables, drinking mint tea.

She was supposed to be studying, but had already abandoned one particularly turgid and archaic text on deep grammar. Fortunately there were plenty of distractions. Ahmed had got cream on his nose and was trying to lick it off with his tongue. Cheyara had soon forgotten the book and was laughing with the others. Then the Cloud alert pinged. Sonya took one look at the message and said:

'Now the shit's really gonna hit the fan!'

Cheyara's Community Cloud interface was pinging with multiple messages, making her skinterface prickle. She opened the News window, which was displaying a familiar group portrait of Expedition One. Two Taiyangren and two Abodans stood against a bluish backdrop, all clad in dark green expedition flight suits. The Taiyangren were, she remembered, named Penguin A Hake and Heron Y Mouse. The other two were Abodans: Madeyeno Osala and Bobby Wong. Bobby crouched below the others, his grin revealing an even row of white teeth, complimenting his immaculate, back-combed black hair.

The news feed switched to a livestream from Nyuki. Osala was giving a report to a shaking camera, against a background of umbrella trees.

'We'd been observing a…situation where there was a House conflict between the Matua and a rogue. The old Matua was killed about ten hours ago, along with her juvenile Matuas. But the new rogue Matua was still struggling for control…. There was a fight in front of the house. At 13:40 Abode time, Robert Wong…Bobby….'

Osala closed her eyes and took a couple of deep breaths.

'Today…Bobby Wong was…killed by the rogue's…. gang…. We…were too late to intercede. We've so far been unable to collect his body and the Taiyangren have agreed to terminate the mission. Recording off.'

Sonya was snapping her fingers in Cheyara's face. Cheyara closed the window and focused on reality. Everyone else was on their feet, and the cafe was emptying. People were milling in the street. More were pouring from complex buildings and even the religious buildings, adding to the jostling caterpillar of objectors.

'Let's go!' Sonya said, and they followed her, joining the throng.

By the time they'd reached Council Square, some were projecting huge holographics of Bobby's face into the air. Cheyara and Sonya were towards the back and Cheyara was jostled and finally wedged against the rough trunk of a date palm.

Several councillors stood on the steps and greeted the objectors. Cheyara struggled to hear them from her position until she switched on her ear speakers, which piped their voices directly into her aural canals. Sonya, who by then was on Ahmed's shoulders, also provided a commentary. The councillors expressed solidarity with the objectors and promised to table a vote on formal withdrawal in the morning. The objectors cheered and then a chant began.

'Get them off! Get them off! Get them off!'

Cheyara and Sonya spent the night in a square occupied by objectors. They sat opposite a group of buddhist monks in saffron and maroon. Spherical Sentinels hung overhead, silently monitoring events, ensuring that they conformed to the Consilience. The pink-hats had also arrived, but for the moment lounged on the steps of the council building. Cheyara knew them: they were friends of her brother. They waved when they first saw her.

A little later two Taiyangren arrived.

Cheyara watched them picking their way through sitting objectors. They ended up sitting on one of the low walls that surrounded the square. They might have been conversing, it was difficult to tell. Most Taiyangren to Taiyangren conversation happened over their Cloud.

Coffees were passed around in the small hours of the morning under an artificial sky emitting fake moonlight. Cheyara was wide awake, buoyed up by caffeine and adrenaline. Hungry to know more, she scoured the news channels, but the analysis was too superficial for her liking.

So she ransacked the Nyuki digital archive. She found a video where Bobby was sitting crosslegged on the ground before a wall of umbrella trees. At the beginning of the recording, he wore a slight, easy smile. There was some sweat on his brow.

'The House is in decline, now,' he said 'The Matua's losing control. She's ill, anyway, so it's happening earlier than normal…. But the juvenile Matuas are growing up….

'I said last time that when the Matua's pheromone output falls off, some workers develop female characteristics and begin laying their own eggs. We call these workers demi-rogues. The Matua…she seeks these worker's eggs out and destroys them. It's a proper witch hunt. The other workers follow the Matua, of course…. The demi-rogues…. It never ends well. We've seen that, first hand…. But all this is common, even routine, for late Autumn. All part of the life-cycle. Just biology….'

He closed his eyes and rubbed his hand over his face. He was looking down at the ground. He cleared his throat and looked directly at the camera, his businesslike tone reasserting itself.

'All of us know what happens next. By the end of autumn,

the social order of the colony has fallen apart. The workers die. The old Matua dies, too. The juvenile Matuas leave the nest and will start new houses next spring. Provided they survive Freeze and Deep Winter….'

Bobby wiped a bead of sweat off his immaculate brow.

'True, full rogues have been seen before. These are workers who complete the transition, becoming Matuas themselves. Unlike demi-rogues, they develop the characteristic protective stings that protrude from their wrists. Epigenetic changes include the longevity to survive the winter and the capacity to mate and lay worker eggs.

'The Matua treats full rogues as household enemies. They're far more threatening to her than demi-rogues. And for good reason. The rogues have the capacity to influence the remaining workers via hormones. They can turn the developing disorder in the House into a war of succession. And a rogue can sometimes win, killing the old Matua and going on to hibernate.'

Someone passed him a hip-flask of water, which he drank, his Adam's apple visibly bobbing. He passed it back and finished.

'This cycle's been a little different. Because of the Matua's disease, we think. Five full rogues have emerged, way more than expected. Way more than average….'

She squeezed an earlobe, closing the window. Sonya and Ahmed's voices were raised as they prosecuted an intense, ongoing discussion. Cheyara listened for a bit, but they were retracing old political ground, and her thoughts began to wander.

Bobby was from Abode 8, in Asali's asteroid belt. Before, he'd just been a face on the news. Watching the videos had revealed his humanity to her. No doubt his cheekbones helped. But more than that, her curiosity had been triggered. She wanted to know more about humble society. It sounded so much more interesting than her current studies.

Later, she huddled in a sleeping bag someone had brought from the University dorms. She soon nodded off, lulled by whispered conversations about her. Dream images of humble faces flickered against the yellow-pink of her eyelids. She was woken at dawn by the Muezzin calling the *Salut Ul Fajr* from the nearby mosque. When she opened her eyes, Ahmed was at prayer.

Later that morning, the motion was tabled early and it was agreed that Nyuki Expedition One was to be cancelled. A collective cheer boomed in waves against the terracotta council building. The noise was so loud that Cheyara's ears rang for hours afterwards. Along with the rest, she felt the warm glow of satisfaction of having preserved an indigenous, intelligent, unique species from harm. Perhaps, she thought, the toxic legacy of Earth could finally be successfully challenged here, among the stars. Perhaps humans could learn from their mistakes. Become compassionate, kinder, less destructively interfering.

At the same time, a part of her was unexpectedly a little disappointed.

·

Afterwards Sonya and she had parted company with the other objectors and spent a long afternoon in bed. They went to sleep very early, and did not emerge until late morning the next day.

'Let's celebrate,' Sonya said, when they were dressing. They wandered hand in hand into the Great Park, spreading towels in a mini-palm grove. Cheyara had brought tubs of food in her rucksack, a fairly safe spiced stew dispensed from the bacterial protein factories, accompanied by tomatoes and salad from Abode 1's hydroponics module. Sonya had brought wine, made with real grapes cultivated in Abode 7. They finished the bottle within the hour. Later they packed up and made a circuit of the park.

It was one of those days when you float and the world seems benign and people are invariably funny and kind. No doubt the wine helped. Then they got lost in the ever-changing inner spaces of the Chuz Lee building-sculpture. They found a slippery seat and necked for a bit, their reflections distorted in the chamber's undulating mirrored surface. Then Sonya said that she was feeling a little nauseous and they looked for the exits. Fortunately, the building sensed their mood and spat them out.

Afterwards Sonya led Cheyara by the hand back to the university dorm, with that too-small bed and that odd stain on the ceiling. They'd both been a little drunk and Cheyara was shaking with desire. They took their time, enjoying the feel of skin against skin. Sonya touched her neck, her back, her breasts. Then she gently parted Cheyara's legs and went down on her. She was skilled with her tongue. Cheyara was staring at the ceiling-stain when she came.

They lay entangled together, listening to their neighbour attempt to sing 'Nottamun Town,' accompanied by guitar. Sonya said that the neighbour had discovered a cache of European folk music recordings in the Earthian archives and had been working their way through the catalogue. At that moment, the neighbour stumbled on another chord. They heard swearing.

They both smiled at one another.

'We did right, didn't we?' Cheyara said. Sonya frowned.

'Of course. Why ask?'

'…I don't know.'

Sonya embraced her, kissing her on the forehead. Her embrace felt like fire, and Cheyara was excited again.

When Sonya was asleep, Cheyara accessed the Nyuki Archive. She'd begun to work her way through the rest of the Expedition Reports.

.

A month later, she'd changed her major to xenoanthropology. It was some time before she plucked up the courage to tell Sonya.

And that was okay, until it wasn't.

13TH JUNE A.Y. 87

MISSION ELAPSED TIME: 293 Days.
LOCATION: NORTHERN SUBCONTINENT 2. NYUKI.
HUMBLE TERRITORY.

Early the next morning, day five in the cycle with Asali rising first, Cheyara woke with a throbbing headache. She'd barely slept and felt as rough as the early days on Nyuki. She ignored the hangover feeling and searched for any new committee notifications. None were forthcoming.

Shit. Heron and she had voted immediately. What was taking the others so long? If the Expedition was to be terminated, she'd rather know at once. The suspense made everything worse.

Late morning, with Asali high in the sky, the clouds thickened, putting Basecamp under a sulphurous, oppressive haze. The forest fell silent and Cheyara could feel tension in the air and tingles on her skin. A weird howling began as the temperature plummeted. The rain began, gently at first and then getting harder. Cheyara felt enveloped in a damp, yellow-green, pungent womb. Gusts of wind buffeted treetops. Thunder grumbled and they both fled to the flier. Rain cascaded down the canopy, coalescing into streams and then rivers, surging down the glass.

Lightning exploded overhead, illuminating Basecamp and surrounding trees. Cheyara hugged herself as Heron watched the reports from the observing weather satellite.

Sometime after Asali noon the rain slackened and the thunder was subsiding to faint, background rumbles. The cloud cover began to break, revealing sky. Biloko had risen, changing the light from yellow to serum where the spectra mixed. The odd shadow effect had emerged, where shadows cast by Biloko appeared yellow and those cast by Asali, red. The Asali shadows were lengthening as the star sank in the west. Insects and amphibians had begun to call again. They ate lunch in silence, watching drops from the awning fall into puddles.

A feeling of deep gloom had descended over Cheyara. This was all her fault. She kicked herself for dropping the gun. She'd handed Sonya the perfect pretext for mission cancellation. And she scarcely dared imagine the fights on the Community Cloud. No doubt her reputation was being dragged through the mud, again. So she faced not only mission cancellation, but community censure.

Terrific.

·

Biloko had passed the zenith, and bathed the world in pink. Cheyara walked slowly along the forest's edge, making a slow circuit of Basecamp. After the rain, the calls of the insects and amphibians rang in her ears. She could see some of the amphibians, clinging to tree trunks, high up, out of reach. A dense mist shrouded the forest interior, complimenting the darkness formed by a thick barrier of summer vegetation. It was as if the forest was deliberately hiding its secrets.

A notification pinged in her visual field. She paused in mid-step, blinked, then accessed the message.

TABLED: Vote on immediate termination of Expedition Two because of firearm incident on A.Y. 12/06/87.
YES: Five.
NO: Four.
ABSTAIN: One.
MOTION REJECTED.

She had to read the message about four times before its implications registered. When they did, she felt as if someone had slapped her hard in the face. The victory was Pyrrhic. A stay of execution, only.

Five 'YES' votes had been counted. The motion was category one, which meant that it needed a majority of six before it could be passed. They'd been saved by a single abstention.

Hang on.

There were only three objectors on committee. That left two 'YES' votes unaccounted for. The fact that two additional committee members had also voted to cancel was almost certainly due to Sonya. Her ten months of service had been put to good use. Machiavelli would've been proud.

But who'd abstained?

Who'd made the decision that had saved the expedition?

'So we carry on,' Heron said, approaching her across a dripping sward. Ey were actually smiling.

Cheyara nodded, feeling dazed. They embraced. Heron smelt of damp earth. A cold raindrop hit the top of Cheyara's head.

'Don't worry. We'll get through,' Heron said, in her ear.

Another notification pinged. Sonya. Words scrolled. Heron and she separated.

She told Heron, then:

'She wants me to use full immersion. Is that okay?'

Heron shrugged.

'Biloko's been behaving itself, so give it a try.'

.

To Cheyara's surprise, they were not on Abode 1 at all. Instead all three had chosen to gather in her old kitchen on Abode 3. Mimesis level was reasonable—a six—and she was hooked up to a micro-drone that would be projecting a holographic image of her that now stood before them. Haptic feedback was minimal, so when she moved she had a slightly drunken sensation, feeling uneven ground beneath her feet and not polished floorboards.

Abode 3 had been landscaped in a traditional Japanese style, resembling parkland that might once have been found

on the outskirts of a city like Tokyo or Kyoto. The house
in which her virtual image now stood was also of Japanese design. Sonya and she had lived there for two years
after graduation. It was Sonya who'd made the suggestion.
They'd been looking for a home of their own, and by chance
she'd discovered it nestling beside a miniature lake in a
toy-sized valley amongst black pines. The place had been
designed as a blend of traditional Japanese architecture
with more modern features. The associated memories were
for Cheyara less than happy ones.

The kitchen in which the three objectors greeted her
was glass-fronted, affording a view of the ornamental lake
beyond. The glass replaced a traditional *shōji* screen of rice
paper. The ceiling was high with genuine bamboo rafters
and the internal architecture was a traditional post and
beam framework.

Cheyara tried to ignore the setting. The kitchen had
also been the site of some of their most ferocious arguments.
Possibly Sonya was trying to remind her of this fact. She
was sitting with the other two objectors at the kitchen table,
with a single foo-dog statue visible to her left on the shelf
behind her. The foo-dog was one of a pair that been broken
in Major Argument Number Four. Cheyara remembered
hurling it onto the wooden flooring and watching it shatter
into a thousand pieces. She couldn't decide whether Sonya
had chosen her seating position deliberately, as a not-so-
subtle reminder of that day.

'So you won,' Sonya said, 'Barely.'

'It's not like that,' Cheyara said, then grit her teeth. No
matter what happened, she mustn't take the bait. Ahmed
was looking down at the table at his clasped hands and
Kimberley gazed at the ceiling whilst fiddling with a lock
of hair.

'You've been lucky, this time.' Sonya was saying, 'But I wouldn't count on that luck holding. Next time, we'll win.'

A livid green alphanumeric string was scrolling across the scene. All three objectors were frozen. Sonya was pouting, Ahmed's mouth was turned downwards like a sad emoji and Kimberley looked bored.

'NOT A-FUCKING-GAIN!'

The scene flickered out, and for a moment Cheyara was caught in the digital void. Then she was back on Nyuki, listening to the patter of steady rain on the canvas.

'What happened?' She said to Heron, who was examining a large botanic specimen on the table with the forefinger of eir synthetic hand. The forefinger was split into a thousand fractal tentacles, roving over the green, pulpy innards.

'I'll check.' Heron straightened up, withdrawing eir hand from the epiphyte. Eir forefinger tentacles retracting, the digit resumed its normal shape. Heron's eyes closed and then ey said.

'That's odd. Stellar weather's quiescent. You shouldn't have had any problems.'

She tried to reconnect, and failed. She tried again. Same result. She wasn't that sorry.

Heron was frowning. Ey asked her to describe exactly what happened. When she told em about the alphanumeric string, Heron's frown deepened. Ey retreated to the flier to conduct more checks.

Cheyara made several fresh circuits of Basecamp. By now the rain was spotting and her already soaked plaits and shoulders only got a little more wet. Still restless, she wandered further, in the direction of the river that flowed immediately East of their base.

In Melt and early spring, the river was a violent cataract, transporting billions of tonnes of meltwater from the mountains. Now it was at its lowest ebb, a cold but relatively narrow watercourse that could be crossed in several places. It was the same course the Matua had followed, several clicks upstream, on her descent from the mountains.

She checked the scanner for any nearby large predators and found none. She sat on the bank in the inadequate shelter of a tree, watching the rain make circles on the steel-grey river surface. Her bottom was cold and soon she'd be soaked through, but it didn't matter.

She used the *Kapalabhati* technique of slow breathing, giving herself mental space. Eventually, she allowed herself to think of Sonya. The situation was bad. The chances of changing her ex's mind was approximately zero. She might possibly have a better chance of a reasonable dialogue with either Ahmed or Kimberley. Ahmed, especially, was committed to rational dialogue.

Or so he claimed.

The trouble was she lacked the energy for any of it. She was terminally bored with Abode politics. Their society was utopian by Earthian standards, but that had not resulted in mental tranquillity. Far from it. The Community Cloud remained a hotbed of vigorous, endless dispute.

Nyuki had shown her how trivial and pointless it all was. Human beings remained irrevocably parochial. Their mayfly lives were spent squabbling over trifles, while the majesty of the cosmos unfolded about them, unseen.

The rain was stopping. She stood up, watching patches of dark blue sky through scudding cloud. The rain had cooled the air and her inhalations were fresh and bracing. The mist to the north had cleared, revealing the far off peaks. Pink snow, illuminated by a setting Biloko, glinted on mountaintops. She needed to appreciate every second here, because it could end at a moment's notice.

Would end, if Sonya had any say. Which she did.

She wandered back in the direction of Basecamp, feeling only a little more at peace with herself.

How was she to know that she was worrying about the wrong thing?

JULY-AUGUST A.Y. 87

LOCATION: NORTHERN SUBCONTINENT 2. NYUKI. HUMBLE TERRITORY.

The last days of summer.

The umbrella trees spread vast, mature, opaque canopies that transformed the forest floor into a cool, green space. Herds of chlorelle and verdiphants browsed across humble territory. The verdiphants demolished whole trees, cracking calciferous trunks open with powerful jaws. The herbivores were followed by packs of medium-sized pack carnivores, with plumage of red and black. This excited Heron. The predators were volpiphones, a rare species in this forest.

Cheyara just kept her distance.

The sands in the hour-glass were running low. Even on heat days, Asali was kicking out less warmth. The effect was even more noticeable when Biloko was below the horizon. The nights were getting colder and on more than one morning Cheyara would crawl out of her tent into dewy mist. One glance at the daily climate reports confirmed that the decline in insolation was slowly accelerating.

Fourteen days before the end of summer, Cheyara met a male.

·

It should have come as no surprise. The drones had been monitoring the hatcheries. But the male was from another House, probably settlement 7 B, seventeen klicks to the east.

Cheyara encountered him one morning when she was walking up the trail from base camp. He was watching her from behind a tree. When he saw her, his face-spiracles formed four Os and he ducked behind the trunk. A moment later, he re-emerged, staring at her and humming to himself. The two lines of chest spiracles also pulsed, as if he'd been running. His long dark red tongue flicked in and out.

Fully mature, his down was dark brown. When he stepped onto the path she saw that he was a head shorter than the average worker. His jaw was broader and squarer and he had a rounded upper lip that barely hid the keratinous cutting edge that substituted for teeth. Prominent claw-like, forked genitalia dangled between his legs. In one hand he held a large beetle, which wriggled in his grip. When he shoved it in his mouth and crunched, crushed carapace and yellow fluid oozed down his chin. His face-spiracles pulsed but emitted no sounds.

'Who are you?' He said then, in almost flawless Standard Earthian. Cheyara was speechless. Males were ejected from the House early. They had no chance to learn much of anything. The offspring of *their* house might, of course, recall the language the Matua had learnt last season. The problem was this individual was almost certainly from another settlement. He should not have been able to speak a word of Earthian.

She wondered for a second whether she'd imagined it.

Then the male pointed a finger at his puffed out chest.

'I...wait.' he said. 'I wait!'

He sniffed the air, jabbed a finger in the direction of the House.

'Soon,' he said. 'Soon.'

Cheyara felt a chill pass over her.

Soon.

In the following days, more males arrived. They lurked amongst the umbrella and stutter trees, watching the pathways close to the House. The workers did not allow them to approach the House itself. More than once Cheyara saw a worker raise eir arms and, emitting a warning hum, chase a horny male from the bushes.

.

Grim news from Abode.

Some time ago, the Taiyangren had sent a warning about some kind of bug that they'd detected in software that was used to mediate Supalite communications. Soon more anomalous 'bugs' were reported, affecting an increasing number of software systems.

As the days passed, the news got worse. The lifts jammed in Abodes 1 and 2, stranding people in the embarkation zones. There were regular power cuts in habitat after habitat.

Augmented Reality had become so plagued by digital phantoms that people were abandoning neural and somatic interfaces for old-fashioned glasses, tablets and screens. Her grandparents might have rejoiced at the latter development. Cheyara just felt ice in her stomach.

There were several accidents with deep space craft and some deaths on Leng. Azleena told her about the Leng deaths, via a video link. Her eyes looked red and she blinked and sniffed between gobbets of conversation. She said that the air filters in two surface rovers had stopped removing carbon dioxide and that the warning notifications had been deactivated. No-one noticed and then they were dead.

'We've lost five people, out on Mordant Plain. So we've been sitting tight, here.'

'Keep safe,' Cheyara said, signing off and cursing her lameness.

After the deaths, no-one was talking about bugs anymore. The general thinking had swung towards computer viruses and worms. The problem was that these were rare. The old, mostly financial, political, criminal reasons for their invention were absent. No-one benefitted from online mayhem. And despite extensive investigation, they couldn't figure out who might be responsible.

·

The regular Nyuki committee meetings offered few solutions, to anything. Interactions had been reduced to audiovisual only. The agenda now concerned only practical matters. This was perhaps unsurprising, because Sonya had been absent the last couple of meetings. She was substituted by Ahmed or Kimberley, who often remained silent while Agara or Magrena spoke. Cheyara was thankful for this, small mercy. She didn't dare query the absence, wary of the Sword of Damocles that the objectors dangled over their heads.

In moments of frustration, she still wished for its permanent removal. But her grandmother had often warned of the dangers of wishes.

22ND AUGUST A.Y. 87

MISSION ELAPSED TIME: 363 days.
LOCATION: NORTHERN SUBCONTINENT 2. NYUKI.
HUMBLE TERRITORY.

Ten humbles formed a semicircle, advancing towards the raiding party. There were six raiders, three in the trees and three on the ground. One of the humbles was jumping up and down on a branch, emitting distress calls. The end of the branch waggled, sending fruit thudding to the forest floor. The other two in the tree threw fruit, which exploded on the ground or occasionally on their rival's heads.

The remaining invaders stood at the foot of the tree, buzzing warnings and gesturing with spread, arachnoid fingers. They'd amassed piles of fruit and had already stowed a surprising quantity in their wicker baskets. The ten humbles from 'her' House carried rocks and crude spears.

Cheyara watched from a safe distance behind the bushes, poised to withdraw if necessary. Diffuse light from Asali and Biloko filtered through cloud, illuminating the scene in yellow-pink.

The defenders hummed one, ominous note, as more fruit struck heads and chests. The humming rose in pitch and all ten of the humbles raised their arms in a choreographed movement. Spreading their hands, with palms facing the invaders, they stamped on the ground.

Aaaaaah!

Stamp, stamp, stamp.

Zzzzzzzzzzzz!

Stamp, stamp, stamp.

By now the fruit pelters had stopped. The ten humbles inscribed large circles in the air.

Zzzzzzzzzzz!

Stamp, stamp, stamp.

The three tree-born humbles dropped onto the ground, joining their companions. All six invaders stood in a line, each planting one foot forward, over and over again. The motion was simultaneous, choreographed.

Stamp, stamp, stamp.

Zzzzzzzzzzzzz!

The semicircle parted. Fruit baskets abandoned, the six raiders began to retreat, following a trail that led past her hiding place. As they passed she took the opportunity to examine them closely. All had patchy fur and parasite scabs. Two were limping, and one carried eir arm awkwardly, as if the shoulder were dislocated. Another wheezed through half-closed breathing spiracles. The trail took them in a southeasterly direction, under clouds the colour of blood.

The defenders continued their ritual stamps, humming and hooting in their wake. The territorial violation had happened early, just prior to the end of summer, when food was still relatively abundant. If this had happened later in the seasonal cycle the outcome might have been very different.

Cheyara sighed, thankful that the confrontation had been bloodless. The ritual displays that were intended to defuse aggression were not always so successful. Later on, with resources dwindling, such incidents could result in mutual slaughter. She'd seen videos of late Autumn fights where the combatants bashed each other's heads in with rocks, or tried to tear each other to pieces with their hands. The ecological disruptions of a waning season did that, destroying stable social patterns, forcing boundary violations, inducing suspicion, fear and violence.

'Chey?' Heron's voice made her jump.

'Yes?'

'Get back here.'

.

Five hours later, in mid-afternoon, Cheyara, footsore with a massive blister on her right big toe, arrived in Basecamp.

Heron had been updating her on the way.

The bottom line: the Supalite was down. The committee was sending messages via radio, which were taking seven hours to reach Nyuki, relayed via a comms satellite in Biloko orbit.

'We've been advised to do an immediate inventory of our supplies,' Heron said, the moment she put her pack down. Cheyara nodded.

'Can I have a coffee first?'

'Be quick.'

They pulled up the checklist and began marking priorities. The most crucial pieces of the equipment—the food synthesisers and the water processors—were fortunately functioning optimally. However, there was a fault on the arm of the robotic surgeon. Heron set one of the repair robots to replace it.

'There's also an emergency synthesiser on the flier,' Heron said, thinking aloud. Cheyara, footsore and exhausted, sat under the awning downing her fourth coffee. Heron was pacing, eir hands dancing as ey flicked through virtual menus invisible to Cheyara.

'I don't get it,' Cheyara said, thinking of the earlier news reports. 'Where are these viruses coming from?'

Heron sat down opposite her, rubbing eir eyes.

'I was talking to one of my colleagues, before the Supalite went down. One of our probes in the Samudra system…. It was trying to contact the Zungui. The Zungui obviously didn't approve. My colleagues think the probe's Supalite got infected.'

'With a virus?'

Heron hesitated. Cheyara chewed her lip.

'No,' said Heron, eventually. 'With something that *writes* viruses.'

'An AI, or something?'

'…right now they're veering towards the "or something."'

'So this is some kind of Zungui weapon?'

Heron shrugged.

'Oh, God,' Cheyara said. 'Is this it? Has the invasion started?'

'I just don't know.'

·

That night, despite her fatigue, she stayed up, watching for breaks in the clouds. She set the telescope up beside her tent. When she began to nod off, she brought her sleeping bag outside. The skies remained cloudy and opaque. The air was muggy, every inhalation tasting metallic and damp. She refused to sleep.

Clear, dammit. Clear!

She needed to see the stars. She had to reassure herself that the universe still looked the same. This, she knew, was completely irrational. A Zungui invasion would probably be invisible for months or years. The seed replicators would activate in the cold darkness of the outer Asali system, quietly assimilating material that would allow growth. And with their tech crippled by viruses, the humans would be sitting ducks.

They might be here already.

Heron's words from the preflight briefing over a year previously came back to her. The truth was that they'd buried their heads in the sand, hoping to avoid an unpalatable reality by collective denial. History had shown this to be hardly a winning strategy.

And now it was too late. Far, far too late.

The skies did not clear that night.

23ND AUGUST A.Y. 87

MISSION ELAPSED TIME: 364 days.
LOCATION: NORTHERN SUBCONTINENT 2, NYUKI.
HUMBLE TERRITORY.

Cheyara awoke outside early in the diurnal cycle, in pre-dawn darkness. She lay on her back, listening to the loud calls of night insects. Stray thoughts and random images churned through her brain. Her leg muscles and shoulders were painfully stiff after yesterday's trek. The blister on her big toe was still sore. Her face was cold. The adjacent forest was shrouded by mist.

Biloko rose first, followed swiftly by Asali. When she

sat up, she found a large yellow and white pseudo-slug crawling on her sleeping bag. She grabbed a tissue from her pocket, picked up the slimy lump and put it on the grass. It uncurled and crawled away. She put her sleeping bag back in the tent and stowed the telescope. The previous night's vigil seemed like an intoxicated dream.

Sipping coffee, she watched the light change amongst the umbrella trees. As the suns rose, the shadows paled and the forest interior revealed itself. Heron was nowhere in sight. Then a new notification pinged. She blinked, accessing the text in a moment. They were ordering immediate, total isolation for the Expedition. For the time being, even radio communications were being 'curtailed.'

The entrance to Heron's tent irised open and ey crawled out. Ey was already fully dressed in khaki overalls and boots, with eir hair in the usual ponytail. Ey nodded to Cheyara then strode over to the flier, climbing inside. Abandoning her coffee, Cheyara scrambled to her feet and ran over to the flier. Heron was running diagnostics.

'They think the comms satellite is infected,' ey said.

They both sat on the grass, waiting for the diagnostic programs to complete. It took several minutes.

'What about the *Msafiri*?'

'They isolated that several hours ago. They think it might have been infected too.'

'Jesus. Can't they send another ship out?'

'Not until they've found out how to neutralise this thing. The AIs figure it's lower risk to have us sit tight.'

Cheyara thought of Azleena's news from Leng. She didn't want to asphyxiate on the way home.

'How long is this going to last?'

Heron shook eir head.

'Heron, I'm frightened.'

'So am I,' Heron said, the fingertips of eir artificial hand brushing the white scars on eir other forearm.

.

It got worse. Towards noon, a robot collided with one of the awning's support poles with such force that the structure shook. Heron saw it and bolted for the flier. Ey clicked eir fingers as the canopy opened.

'Come on, come on!' Ey hopped up two of the steps and leant over into the cockpit, ripping off a cover with eir bionic hand and throwing it on the seat. Cheyara watched as ey then poked eir finger into an interface, turning the display indicators dark.

'Should have done that hours ago.'

Ey ran to the first container, yanking open the door and ducking inside. Cheyara hovered at the entrance. Red lights were flickering on several instruments. Ey was swiping through displays invisible to her.

'We ran diagnostics,' she said, feeling faint. She breathed deeply, stifling panic.

'We've been careless,' Heron said, poking the air, 'And the diagnostics are obviously useless.' Cheyara squeezed a skinterface so that she could sync with Heron. Heron glanced at her. A wall of green alphanumerics was spooling in front of her nose.

'That might not be a good idea, either.'

Shit. The possibility that their somatic and neural interfaces might also be corrupted had never occurred to her. She closed her eyes and flipped her mental 'off' switch, then squeezed a thigh skinterface for the required number of seconds. The Augmented Reality display indicator disappeared from the top right of her visual field. Her neural lace was now inert.

She opened her eyes, feeling naked, exposed. Heron had already removed eir bionic hand and placed it on top of one of the sealed crates.

'Are you going to be okay? Without that?' Cheyara nodded at the discarded hand.

'I have a spare.'

Ey pushed past her, moving to the second container.

'How were things?'

'Totally fucked.'

.

The damage:

The software of the machines in Containers 1 and 2 had been corrupted by viruses. This included the large surgical robot, two food synthesisers, two water processors and one waste converter. Also included were four robots and several crucial scientific instruments. They tried restoring the affected equipment to factory settings, but this failed. So the machines were effectively irreparable, dead. Heron said that a software patch, transmitted through the Supalite, had probably acted as a trojan horse.

They were a little luckier with the third container. A lightning strike had fried an antenna, which Heron had only just replaced. This meant that the software patch had not been installed in the equipment.

'The emergency food synthesiser in the flier also seems unaffected,' Heron said, 'as far as I can see.'

'What about the flier itself?' Cheyara said. Heron gnawed a nail.

'As far as I know, it's clean. I've rescanned and I can't find anything.'

'But you said the diagnostics were useless!'

Heron shrugged.

·

Side by side, they slumped in the flier's shadow. The suns hung over trees. It would not be long until the parent stars fell below the horizon, plunging the forest into darkness. Cheyara felt numb. Her ears rang with a terrible inner silence. She'd never understood how comforting the constant hum of the neurosomatic interface operating systems had been. Now they were gone, there were only the sounds of her own body.

Fortunately, this silence was not unprecedented. When she'd been a kid, Unyime had insisted upon the observance of 'Silent Sundays,' which had meant a total deactivation of all electronic media, including somatic and neural interfaces. There were also times when the church held retreats, and whole weeks were spent avoiding any sort of Cloud connection. At the time, she'd resented this observance, as kids do. But in hindsight, the experience had been a blessing.

Looking back it was obvious that her grandmother's outlook on technology had been conditioned by the horrors she'd witnessed on Earth. She'd wanted her descendants to retain the capacity to live free. Even as a kid, Cheyara understood, really. She'd been shown archive video from the Singularity Zones of the end times. Every school kid had. That horrible footage of grim, gaunt lines of human beings, each neurally linked, moving as one.

So she could understand their fear. Besides, the observance had been bearable and in some ways, although she'd never admitted it, a relief. But there is all the difference in the world between a voluntary abstinence and an enforced isolation.

The suns sunk and the incessant insect symphony grew louder. She found herself jumping at animal calls. The umbrella trees rose before her, suddenly menacing. She recalled a scene from an ancient film she'd watched with her grandmother. Snow White lost in the woods. Trees with claws, reaching. Eyes in darkness. Suddenly those primal, childhood terrors seemed very real.

A shadow was moving through the undergrowth. Heart thrumming in her ears, her muscles stiffened, primed against possible attack. Adrenalin surged in her gut, nauseating her. But Heron placed a restraining hand on her shoulder.

Flora emerged from the trees, skirting around an overturned, inert robot. Ey squatted before them, extended a spidery hand and placed it on Cheyara's knee. Cheyara caught her breath, absorbed by Flora's almost subliminal hum and adenoidal breath.

·

Flora stayed with them throughout that first night.

SEPTEMBER-DECEMBER A.Y. 87

LOCATION: NORTHERN SUBCONTINENT 2, NYUKI. HUMBLE TERRITORY.

Autumn. The decline in insolation was accelerating. The polar seas would be refreezing. Heat days no longer seemed worthy of the name, red and yellow days were at most pleasantly warm. But there was still a little time of warmth left. Autumn was a far longer season on Nyuki than it had been on Earth. Official onset this cycle was the 28th August 87. The first day of Freeze was April 21st the next year.

The forest was changing. In the cool mornings it was dank, damp and smelt of mould. Fruiting bodies had begun to appear. Mushrooms popped out of leaf litter and through the moss on fallen tree stumps. Late, modest, autumn flowers bloomed. These were too small for the humble workers, who'd swapped to a diet of fruit.

Offplanet comms were still down. Heron, using an emergency mobile satellite transceiver independent of the flier, was unable to link with the *Msafiri*, Abode or eir own people. They continued regular equipment inventories. Heron winced at every malfunction.

In the absence of somatic interfaces, they were reduced to using AR glasses and a sheaf of disposable tablets that had been stored in the back of container 3. It was like going back to the olden days on Earth. Fortunately, the local drones still seemed to work, although it took a little fiddling to sync them with the glasses. The tablets were even worse. Manual operation seemed so clunky after her neural lace. Cheyara's fingers felt like sausages at first.

Comms have to be restored soon, Cheyara thought, tapping away. *Unless the invasion has begun….*

She found herself scanning the night sky for the *Msafiri*. The orrery program predicted the passes. Thanks to the stealth armour it was magnitude 5 or so, but spottable in their small telescope. The dim speck of light offered little comfort.

Field studies, as ever, offered distractions. As the days and weeks passed, Cheyara found herself checking for changes in the worker's behaviour, especially in her informants. For a while, she saw none. Household business continued as usual.

The Matua was a different story. She was visibly ageing. There was grey in her thinning fur, her muscles had shrunk and her stomach sagged. She walked with a slight stoop. Despite this, she retained a wiry strength. Once Cheyara saw her lift a worker with one arm, flinging em against a wall.

The Matua was also becoming restless. She was laying less and spending more time patrolling the House and its immediate environs. A retinue of workers trailed behind her like groupies.

One red day Cheyara was crouching in the empty hatchery, watching Flora clean rotting straw out of the 'pens.' The Matua entered with her trailing retinue, her face-spiracles dilating as she sniffed the air. She paused, looming over Flora but saying nothing. Then she kicked em in the stomach. Flora cowered gasping, eir arms flung in the air in a supplicatory gesture.

The Matua's stings were out, with a drop of venom at the tips. The Matua ran the tip of one sting slowly across Flora's back, pausing at the neck. Flora didn't move. The

Matua began speaking in low whistles and hums. She held the sting at an eye and hissed.

Then she straightened up.

Cheyara shrank into the corner as the burbled monologue erupted into a loud buzzing, clicking, humming rant. As she spoke the Matua jabbed her protruding, sharp stings at Flora's head. By now, Flora was grovelling with eir chest pressed onto the floor. The Matua struck eir back with her stick and stalked from the room. Flora began to shake. Ey were emitting a low, continual hum.

Afterwards, Cheyara bent over to help Flora to stand, but Flora pushed her away. She waited until Flora was on her feet before she quietly withdrew.

She mulled over the incident back at Basecamp. She'd become too close to Flora. That was a problem because it had blinded her to something very obvious. Flora had been part of an early spring brood of six. On a tablet, Cheyara opened the files of her contemporary siblings. Three were now dead and the remaining two, Poppy and Wallflower, were full-time foragers. Her hand flew to her mouth as she brought up recent drone portraits. Poppy and Wallflower now had shrunken, wrinkled prune-faces. Wallflower had a cataract and Poppy was almost bald. The rapid ageing was a cellular effect, probably triggered by the decline in insolation. Worker longevity was bound by sunlight and cell-death.

Fumbling with the tablet, she opened Flora's file. The most recent portrait was two days old. Flora looked pretty much as ey had done eight months previously. Eir face remained plump and youthful and eir black eyes were clear.

No, that wasn't quite true. Ey didn't look exactly the same. Ey had become more muscular, thicker set. Eir down had darkened a shade, to a deep red-brown. This was in contrast to the average worker, whose down became bleached with age. Cheyara nodded, swiping the files shut. This complicated matters. The problem was that there was nothing she could do.

·

In the ensuing days, the reaper hovered over the House. Cheyara watched the funeral processions. The humbles practised excarnation. When a worker died in or near the house, they would weave flowers and leaves into eir fur and carry the corpse to a nearby charnel ground, where they would deposit the body, perform a short ceremony and withdraw. The translation software gave Cheyara the gist of the eulogies. One translation:

[Worker name] one part now [is in] whole again.
Lift arms to say that a part is whole.
The whole was [never?] [nothingness?] so cannot be a part.
Part never [separate? Distinguished?]
Apart now part [Dismember? Scatter?]
Wave moving [pond? lake?] up moving down there then [gone? nothingness?]
We [wave together? pond image, puddle?] then gone.

Cheyara spent many hours puzzling over these utterances. She wished that Leyon were present, because he might have understood better. One thing she noticed was that, except when they were physically threatened, the humbles seemed unafraid of death. Nor did she ever see them mourn.

If they didn't mourn, what was the purpose of the funeral procession? Cheyara eventually concluded that it was more about community hygiene and possibly the restoration of order than grief or sorrow.

Cheyara quizzed Flora about this, but those conversations proved dead ends. Flora would say little and then lapsed into silence. This was a moment of frustration for both of them, as if each harboured incommunicable thoughts. Besides, Flora seemed distracted these days and Cheyara noticed that ey now spent more time outdoors, avoiding the Matua.

Time was running short, for both of them. Biological cycles, responsive to declining light, were winding down. The previously emerald forest was turning yellow and brown. The ice was on its way.

29TH DECEMBER A.Y. 87

MISSION ELAPSED TIME: 492 days.
LOCATION: NORTHERN SUBCONTINENT 2. NYUKI.
HUMBLE TERRITORY.

Pickup day. In theory. *Incommunicado,* after four months of isolation, they'd neglected to make even preliminary preparations. She stayed at Basecamp all day with Heron. That morning was intensive training. Heron had revised the drill rota some time back, and once more, Cheyara was practising field medicine. Today, how to treat a punctured lung with no surgical robot available. Just watching the training video was enough to tell her it wasn't a scenario that she ever wanted to face.

In the afternoon, she helped Heron use the only

functioning large constructor to experiment with building emergency winter shelters. The first pieces were printing now. Cheyara packed the constructor with stray branches, and Heron took the new wall sections and glued. Eventually a vaguely polyhedral dung-coloured shelter sat in the middle of Basecamp. Heron was already shaking eir head.

'No that won't do.' Ey marched into the third container and emerged wielding a spade. Ey began to dig a hole.

'Perhaps we could build a partially buried structure, before the ground freezes,' Ey said, turning a sod with the spade.

'There'll be snow, too,' Cheyara said, remembering her mountain survival training, 'We could dig a shelter.' She sat cross-legged on the ground. 'But there are still months to go before Freeze! They're bound to have sorted this out by then!'

Heron gave her a look.

'And what if we *have* been invaded?' Ey said. 'You need to look at our clothing situation.'

She sighed and nodded.

·

It was a heat day, unexpectedly warm. Towards evening they sat together under the awning. These days, they spent more and more time together. Nyuki seemed much more alien now they were isolated from the larger body of humanity. She even found herself missing Sonya. She also wondered how Heron coped, with the deactivation of eir Cloud link to the Taiyangren. She'd heard that they were more dependent on this link than Abodans. Outwardly, ey seemed unaffected, but it was hard to tell.

Night fell and the glow-globes illuminated, attracting

large insects. Cooler evenings had seen the arrival of large, green-bodied insects with lacy wings the size of small plates. Heron was reclining in eir chair, arms folded over eir chest, watching the insects drift in and out of the small oasis of light.

Then, to her surprise, ey started talking about Expedition One.

'In the spring and for most of the summer, things were fine,' ey said. 'We became enchanted by the forest. The humbles were mostly friendly. We only encountered large predators three times. The worst injuries were stings, cuts and grazes. Nyuki seemed like Eden to us. For a while we forgot that this was just appearance….

'Of course all four of us knew what to expect, at the end of the household life-cycle. We'd literally written the book! But it was all from afar, via drones. Some things can't be known in that way. Some things take first hand experience….'

Ey sighed, and scratched eir scar. An especially large insect settled on one of the awning's support poles.

'The first indication of trouble was squabbles in the hive. Bobby arrived one morning and two workers were rolling around on the floor. They had to be separated by their peers. Soon more fights were breaking out all over the place. Workers were going truant, foraging parties not bothering to return. Other workers became preoccupied with their own projects, daubing the walls with…images.

'It was like the community went a little mad. The humbles…they were tolerating us, but we began to keep our distance. Madeyeno…she wanted nothing to do with it. She effectively went on strike, staying at Basecamp…. By mid-Autumn, about this time in the season, Bobby was the only one who dared get close to the House. Penguin and I spent most of our time in the forest, avoiding the House…. My people were negotiating with your council, debating withdrawal…. If only they'd reached a consensus a little sooner….

'By then we'd seen several workers with female characteristics. And full rogues, with wrist stings. Those ones…. Well, they began to attract…followers. The Matua…she was losing her grip, and she knew it. She got mean. We all watched the livestreams from the House. She started an active campaign to root out and kill any potential usurper….

'But she was also ill, weak, diseased. She lost control early. So that season was a bad one. *Five* Full Rogues! I can't tell you how bad it was for us. The anthropology team had four humble informers, every single one of whom was killed in the House battles. Three were stung to death and a fourth…well….

'That was Bobby's mistake. He'd become…fond of his informers. He'd developed attachment, despite the fact that he knew…that we all knew what would happen at Summer's end…. But there was one other mistake that he wasn't responsible for. That was our collective responsibility. One that we should have seen coming.

'On the morning that it…happened, Bobby was monitoring the remote drone feeds. He said…. Well, I reviewed them later for the enquiry. They showed a fight breaking out in the hatchery. The old Matua had barricaded herself in and was being defended by several of her workers who'd made crude spears from tree branches. Bobby recognised one of our informants holding a spear. Bobby…wanted to go and negotiate. I told him that this was foolish, that we had no choice but to let things take their course, just as if we weren't there. All we could do was observe. All we *should* do was observe.

'Bobby said "I can't just stand by and do nothing."

'"Yes you can!"'

'He really thought he could stop this. "They have their own culture," I remember him saying, "They're evolving. Surely they can change!"'

'But that is not our business. You can't—*shouldn't*—force another culture to change. Anyway, I remember him setting off down the path to the House. Madeyeno begged him not to go…. He didn't listen, of course. It was crazy.

'"It's okay," he said, "We're immune. I'll be fine."'

'When he said that, we'd been holed up for weeks and weeks in Basecamp. I thought it might be bullshit at the time. But it was true that the team had been physically present when several of the fights broke out. Each time, they'd been totally ignored and the aggressors had focused upon their own species. Bobby figured it was something hormonal, that human biochemical signatures didn't razz them up. But Bobby couldn't know that our—*his*—immunity had already been compromised.

'I saw it all from the remote drones….' Heron hesitated, then activated a file on a tablet and swiped it open. Ey passed her the tablet.'I don't suppose it matters now if you see this.'

The images flickering before her showed the front of the House from a viewpoint about ten metres above the forest floor. The clearing was visibly the same but the vegetation had grown in a visibly different way. As for the House: by this time, she'd become familiar with every wall-facet, every timber, every mural of the current version. This House was subtly different, although clearly built over the same foundations and between the same umbrella trees.

Still, it was familiar. She'd studied the House images from Expedition One in preparation for the flight. The artwork on the walls formed a record of the peak and descent of a seasonal culture. Some of the oldest murals were still visible on the walls, which were now broken by roughly-torn holes. Those older murals showed green plants, gambolling chlorelles, flowers, trees, flitters and stars against a cerulean sky. These were like the fading memories of a happier time, obscured by newer 'projects,' clumsy zigzag daubs in red and brown that formed patterns that she didn't quite like.

Even these projects had been defaced by graffiti. One prominent piece showed a stick-Humble dancing on broken eggshells—an obscene image in their culture. Another cartoonish piece of graffiti showed one stick-figure stinging another. The aggressor's face spiracles were round circles, indicating shouting, presumably a victory-cry. The vanquished was reeling and eir...*her* eyes were shut.

A movement distracted her from the murals. Humbles poured out of all three ground floor exits. The drone dipped, the image blurring before it focused on the surging crowd pooling in the clearing. Some carried short spears, others stone knives, others rocks or sticks. The crowd was emitting loud, angry buzzing, shoving and jostling one another. Presently a circle formed in the middle and one worker was thrown to the ground. Ey was crying out with plaintive hums and flailing in the air. Eir fur was caked with blood.

A nasty sight, but not unusual for the end of summer. The crowd surged forward, a relentless tide of angry people, trampling the hapless worker.

'Did Bobby see that...?'

Heron shook his head.

'He'd already left. That's what we saw from Basecamp.'

Ey slowed the clip as a human figure appeared on the edge of the clearing. A lithe male in khaki overalls with combed-back, black hair. Bobby. His face was flushed and sweaty and he was panting.

The moment he appeared, the crowd undulated and spears were raised. The humming increased to fever pitch. One humble threw a rock, which struck the side of Bobby's head. Bobby fell to the ground, on his knees. Blood gushed from his wound, splashing on the dust. The humbles raced forward, abandoning the sprawled form of their previous victim. Cheyara saw swinging arms and stabbing spears....

'Stop!' She said, 'Stop!'

Heron reached over and stopped the playback.

'Sorry.'

Cheyara shook her head.

'It's okay. What happened after...?'

She already knew. They all did. But she needed to hear it from Heron.

'Well, he was certainly dead. His life-sign monitor told me that. So I...I had to go and get him. No-one else would, not even Penguin. Afterwards...the humbles left him outside the House and normally, they're not very active at night.... Fortunately...if that's the right word, this happened at the end of a heat day, so I had a full night as cover....'

'You went to get him.'

'Yes. But I made another mistake. One that was almost fatal for me.... These were not normal times. I went too soon....'

Ey closed eir eyes, remembering.

'It was a little chill on the path, in the forest. There was already dew on the vegetation.... The night was quiet, too. Some insect calls, but nothing like midsummer... Anyway, just to be safe, I made sure that I was exuding humble hormone "friend" signals.

'Because even then, we suspected.... I felt warmth as I

approached the clearing. The whole house was radiating heat. I saw licks of flame through the front entrance. I heard buzzing. Bobby's poor crushed body had been propped up on the House wall. His face…what was left of it… was covered in blood.

'I was as quiet as possible, but they must have heard me…a crowd surged from the doors. They carried stones. They were so *fast*….' Heron was cradling eir scarred arm.

'You were hit.'

'Yes. My arm was… shattered by a full rogue. By *the* full rogue. I was in shock but I ran into the forest. I think I got lost. I fell and felt too weak to stand up. But I heard someone shouting. Then I passed out. Penguin found me. Ey'd followed me at a distance, tracking my GPS position but not daring to get too close to the House. Ey got me back to Basecamp and the surgical robot performed the emergency amputation…. I was never so grateful for Taiyangren technology…. I opted for a field graft, and the machine printed a new forearm and hand for me….' Ey wiggled the fingers of eir organic, replacement hand.

'What about Bobby?'

'The humbles left him where he was. No-one dared attempt another retrieval…. We thought of sending a stealth robot but that was vetoed by the committee…. So the scavengers got him…. Although he must have been indigestible to them, with his alien biochemistry….'

Cheyara nodded. She remembered the outrage, that there wasn't even a body. Sonya and she had attended the inquest at the council building, which was packed out. Bobby's family had appeared and publicly condemned the council, condemned the Nyuki committee, condemned Expedition One. She would never forget the sight of Bobby's parents, openly weeping. She swallowed.

'What happened next?'

'It was…three weeks before the relief shuttle arrived. Three weeks, with three survivors holed up in Basecamp…. You know, we never found out why he'd been attacked like that. But I have some ideas. He was biologically male…. I think that for most of the season that didn't matter, but at summer's end…. Maybe it was the testosterone he was exuding. Some kind of hormonal contamination. Maybe it was something else. I don't know….'

'But you were attacked, too….'

'By that time I think that the humble community had decided that we were a threat. Remember that they're not animals. They're not just operating on instinct. They've evolved the capacity to make choices….'

'It must have taken a lot of courage to come back. I mean, the others never did…. And what about the risk that the Matua would decide that you were still an enemy…?'

'Well, we ran those simulations….'

'Yes.'

'The most likely outcome was that we'd be accepted, at least in the earlier phase of the life-cycle. And this time we were supposed to be gone before it got nasty.'

'But you didn't know for sure.'

'No. We didn't know for sure.'

JANUARY-MARCH A.Y. 88

LOCATION: NORTHERN SUBCONTINENT 2. NYUKI. HUMBLE TERRITORY.

Cut off from her people, time fell through her fingers. Heat dwindled as the season ebbed. By that time she'd spotted several demi-rogues. Each sported an additional genital slit and two wrist-stubs, malformed stings. When she first saw one on the livestream feed, Cheyara, cued by Heron's tale, expected an immediate response from the Matua. She was quite surprised when this didn't happen. Instead days passed with the routine of the House apparently unaffected. The newly female were not rejected by the community, continuing their duties as workers.

At first, Cheyara was almost but not quite lulled into calm. The events at the House this Autumn had not so far matched the ferocity of the last. But there was no doubt that the workers were more irritable than previously. There were also more deaths, once ten in as many days. The older workers were not replaced because the Matua had stopped laying worker eggs. The family now numbered less than sixty.

Watching the funeral processions became oppressive, but she felt duty-bound to attend as many as possible. The charnel-ground was now covered in fungi and stank of rotting meat. Carrion insects hovered over torn remains that writhed with larvae. The workers did not seem to care, slinging the bodies onto the pile and turning their backs. They'd abandoned any further attempt at ceremony.

Most of the hatcheries were now empty, with only

one large chamber still in use. This was reserved for the juvenile Matua, which were more or less the same colour as the worker children but heavier-set and with sting-buds on their wrists.

The Matua patrolled less, spending much of her time in the hatchery, watching over her new, special children. Her preoccupation was a possible reason for her apparent non-reaction to the demi-rogues. Cheyara noticed, however, that the newly-female workers never entered the hatchery.

Then the transgression came.

It was a chilly morning after a frost and Cheyara was still halfway through her breakfast, swiping through the surveillance stream of the previous full night. The recording showed the forest in deep fluorescent, infrared greens. The House was about two hundred metres from the drone's position, but hidden by trees. Several bright lumps sat slumped against the trees. As she watched, one moved, scratching its rump.

The closest male was hugging himself against the night cold. The drone hovered near his face, showing half-closed eyelids. She'd seen this before. In polar contrast to the hyperactive workers, the males spent an inordinate amount of time asleep or in a semi-trance, softly buzzing and humming to themselves.

She swiped to a later time frame. With dawn, light began to seep into the forest. Something moved in the gloaming. She flipped from infrared to normal vision. The nearest male's eyes were open and he was sniffing the air. He stood, stamping on the ground as his head roved back and forth. As he sniffed, his gaze settled on a figure moving through the trees. The males began to emit an excited hum.

The demi-rogue moved quietly, with stealth. When the male began his mating-call, her pace quickened and soon she was face to face with him. Both parties now sang, but quietly. The male followed the demi-rogue's lead, crooning softly.

The mating was brief, almost perfunctory. Afterwards, the demi-rogue didn't hang around and the male sank to his haunches, watching her departure. He hummed to himself through pulsing face-spiracles.

'The first of the pretenders.' Heron said, peering at the tablet over her shoulder.

'That's not funny.'

'It wasn't meant to be. She'll be after them all, now.'

*

The third autumn gale came before the consequences could arrive. In full night furious winds blew heavy rain onto the forest. Cheyara and Heron hid in the flier, which shook with the gusts. The wind battered the trees, flinging torn branches and foliage everywhere. In the morning, they had to retrieve their tents from halfway across Basecamp.

Then they checked the remaining functional equipment in Container 3. They were both relieved to find all of it undamaged. Their lives hung on the continuing function of the food synthesisers.

'What's their operational life?' Cheyara said, as Heron finished the inspection.

'In theory? Ten years. If you replace the filters.'

'I hope we're not here that long.'

'Do you really think we could survive the whole winter?'

Afterwards, she wandered the forest. It was a heat day and the twin suns cast their blended red-gold light on wreckage. The air was cool and there were large puddles everywhere. Withered golden brown giant umbrella tree leaves lay in heaps against tree trunks. She had to scramble over large, torn branches. Then she came across a dead male humble with blank, black eyes and his head twisted right around. Insects already crawled on his face. She covered him in leaves.

She soon discovered, via a drone livestream, that the House had been damaged. The wind had torn several holes in the walls. This late in the season, the humbles were unlikely to repair them.

.

One morning, six days later, she saw the remaining workers milling outside the entrance. There were shouts coming from inside. Cheyara instantly recognised the Matua's shrill buzz-hums.

She flipped to an inside view and soon discovered the reason for the Matua's tantrum. The translation was providing a running commentary at the bottom of the feed.

Who laid the bad eggs? Who laid the bad eggs?

The Matua was holding an egg in her hand. Workers cowered before her. Furiously, she threw the egg on the floor. The egg bounced and hit a wall.

Cheyara quickly searched the room's livestream timeline. She soon found the egg's source. The fertilised pretender had created a small nest behind discarded pots in a store room. Recorded footage showed her furtively piling straw behind the pots and grunting softly as she laid.

Cheyara abandoned the tablet and ran up the forest track. She needed to witness this for herself. As she ran, she wondered whether she was being as foolish as Bobby.

Despite the danger, she still she felt compelled to bear witness.

When she arrived, she saw two workers setting down the summer throne. The workers festooned the throne with seed-heads, yellow grass and dried flowers. Others scattered more dried flowers in a wide circle as the remaining family filed out of the House.

Cheyara resisted the urge to go any closer. Instead she remained in the shadow of the umbrella trees. She needed to be able to escape quickly if necessary. She scanned the visible workers and couldn't see Flora. That was both a worry and a relief. Another worker carried a pot of eggs out of the House and placed them beside the throne.

The Matua was the last to emerge. She walked with a slight hobble and leant on a stick. Despite this she remained a formidable presence. Her appearance triggered a loud, continuous, ritual hum from the household. The Matua sat upon her outdoor throne. The demi-rogue was dragged out by a loyal worker and thrown on the ground before the Matua.

Cheyara was so mesmerised that she barely registered Heron's arrival. Ey said nothing but put a restraining hand on her shoulder. Cheyara felt a little stronger with eir presence. It would somehow have been worse, seeing this alone.

The Matua was speaking now in a loud voice that echoed off the trunks of the umbrella trees. The pretender grovelled at her feet, begging for mercy. The Matua picked up the pot of eggs and upended them. She flung the pot, which smashed into pieces on the compacted ground. The eggs rolled. The Matua crushed one, then another underfoot. The pretender screamed, a shrill high-pitched discordant buzz that made Cheyara's ears ring. The Matua loomed over her, her feet still covered in egg goo and fragments of shell. Then she gestured to two loyal workers. The workers grabbed the demi-rogue, who wriggled in their grasp, buzzing and clicking in distress. The Matua struck her across the face with her sting. The loyalists let go of the pretender, who staggered on the ground, clutching her face. The Matua was punching her now, stinging over and over again. The demi-rogue shivered in a foetal position as her face, shoulders and chest ballooned with stings. When it was over the Matua swooned onto the throne. The humming subsided and the crowd began to break up.

Heron was tugging at Cheyara's arm.

For a few moments, Cheyara resisted the tugs. She still couldn't see Flora. Eventually, she relented and let Heron lead her back to Basecamp.

.

Heron decided that it was prudent to stick to Basecamp. After witnessing the situation at the House, Cheyara could only agree.

All they could do now was watch via drone as the tragedy unfolded. Cheyara spent many hours poring over the feeds. She felt somehow compelled to bear witness to these terrible events.

Demi-rogues were still emerging. Cheyara learned to spot them at a glance. The most obvious sign was the opening of a second, genital slit. Still, they did not always seem to comprehend their state, pursuing their duties until they were noticed. Workers once set upon a new female whilst she was filling pots full of water by the river. Another was forcibly ejected from the House by a mob, who bombarded her with handfuls of shit.

Flora remained absent from the House. Cheyara did a search of the video archive and found that the last drone sighting had been eight days previously. Flora had been on a foraging trip, but there was no record of eir return. Cheyara cursed herself. This was something else that she'd failed to notice. If Flora had not returned home then ey were probably dead.

The prosecution of the new females escalated. The Matua ordered that any rival should be immediately impounded until she was ready to personally deal with the transgressor. The remaining workers converted one of the store rooms into a makeshift prison. Soon the prison housed three, then four demi-rogues. Cheyara watched them on the feeds. For the most part, they sat against the wall, staring into space or buzzing to comfort themselves.

'That's new,' Heron said, 'The last Matua never did that.'

'I know.' Cheyara chewed a nail. There was no obvious reason for the change in behaviour.

Possibly it had something to do with personality. This Matua was tough, cunning and had surrounded herself with loyal workers. The Matua had also maintained a persistent if declining level of hormonal control, which suppressed worker ovulation and ensured loyalty. This was different from last season, when the Matua had weakened early, through disease. But the appearance of demi-rogues was a sign that this control was waning. Although perhaps significantly, a full rogue had not yet emerged.

Except, Cheyara thought, *a full rogue has already emerged, hasn't she?*

Maybe she'd had the sense to disappear.

She hoped so. She hoped that Flora still lived. But in her absence it looked likely that next season's House would be built by one of the juvenile Matuas. They were approaching maturity, their growth spurts no doubt triggered by Asali's tanking insolation. Cheyara could see them on the hatchery feed, singing to their ageing Matua. Some of the oldest looked almost pubertal. Soon they would leave the House on a hunt for a male, seeking fertilisation before the true cold came. After mating the new Matua would journey to the Mountains and with luck reach their hibernation caves before conditions became too severe. So it was a race between biology and ice.

One night, after Asali had set and the forest had plunged into chill darkness, Cheyara became alerted to a movement on one of the drone feeds. At first she thought 'male,' but they travelled with uncharacteristic purpose and stealth. The two humbles moved arm in arm as they hurried down an old foraging track.

She moved the drone down for a closer look. The pair were moving directly away from the House, passing two males without a pause. The males buzzed feebly in their semi-torpor, but did not pursue.

Cheyara was intrigued: she'd never seen anything quite like this. The drone followed the humble's progress as they moved deeper into the autumn forest. They looked like they were heading in a very specific direction. Cheyara felt a lightness in her chest and her pulse raced. This was something new, something potentially significant. She thought of alerting Heron, but she didn't want to take her eyes from the feed.

The demi-rogues seemed to know exactly where they were going. They came to a fork in the track, hardly hesitating before picking one trail. Cheyara had already opened the map, which showed two green blinking dots moving up the white trail line. She nodded in satisfaction. The trail ultimately led to the foothills of the mountains.

The foothills….

It couldn't be. It wasn't possible. And yet….

A red alert light was blinking on the tablet. Another drone had registered something unusual at the House. She swiped up the feed. Four workers were emerging, stepping over the debris from the House's crumbling walls. This nocturnal emergence was also very unusual. The workers were sniffing the air. Two carried spears, and two large stone hand-axes. They followed the same trail the fugitives had taken.

Cheyara alerted Heron.

'We've got to help them!' she said.

'You know we can't.' Heron said.

'But this….'

'We can't.'

Instead they followed the pursuit remotely. The hunters— it was difficult to think of them as anything else—seemed to know exactly where the two demi-rogues had been. When they came to the fork they followed the correct path without hesitation. They could probably smell the transgressors.

The hunters caught up with the hunted halfway up the slope of the first hill. They surrounded them and…well, it was over quickly. The demi-rogues couldn't even beg for their lives.

Cheyara turned off the feed.

'I'm not sure how much more of this I can take.'

'Me neither.'

24TH MARCH A.Y. 88

MISSION ELAPSED TIME: 578 days.
LOCATION: NORTHERN SUBCONTINENT 2. NYUKI.
HUMBLE TERRITORY.

Dawn on heat day. That morning there was a heavy frost on withering ground herbs. They were almost three months past pickup day, and still not a peep from the outside universe.

A full-sized winter shelter had been constructed in the middle of Basecamp, half sunk in the ground and covered with an insulating layer of soil. Cheyara had already tried sleeping a night inside. It was very cramped, and would no doubt stink after months of human habitation. But there was no choice. They'd been forced to complete it before the ground froze.

Today, Heron was in the flier, searching the comms channels manually on the mobile transceiver. This was futile, something the onboard AI could do in an instant. But ey searched all the same. Cheyara had pulled on a coat and sat under the awning, all motivation gone.

The umbrella trees were now almost entirely bare and the trunks were exuding the thick, grey rind of cryobark that would protect them against extreme subzero temperatures. A chill wind was blowing. The frost-rimed underbrush had largely decayed, consumed by the moulds and fungi that had given the forest a rank, moist smell.

Then the Matua herself turned up at the edge of their camp. Heron and Cheyara went to greet her, but kept their distance. The Matua was accompanied by her worker retinue, who slouched either side of their monarch. Her fur was now entirely grey and matted, except for the white fur mask that fringed her withered face. She carried her carved stick, but her step was vigorous and her dark eyes were sharp. She stank of excrement and old urine.

She prodded her stick at them.

'She has been here!'

'No-one has been here,' Heron said. Ey was wearing a nonlethal weapon hung from eir belt, liberated from the stores. Cheyara was similarly armed.

The Matua was sniffing the air.

'No, I can smell her! She mated and she came here. You must let me have her!' The painfully-thin, prune-faced workers raised their spears and shook them, humming with anger.

'No-one has been here,' Cheyara said, parroting Heron. The tips of her fingers brushed the weapon.

'We will search!' The Matua said.

'You will not.' Cheyara said. 'And we cannot help you. It is not allowed.'

One of the workers flung a stone. It skimmed past Cheyara's head and landed with a dull thud behind her. The Matua's stings were fully extruded, with drops of venom welling on the tips. Cheyara resisted the urge to retreat. They had the antivenom, of course, but the poison was lethal to humans and acted fast.

'You are no longer welcome on my land,' The Matua said. 'You must be gone by tomorrow.'

Then she lashed out. They both leapt back, but the Matua was too fast. Heron fell to eir knees, clutching eir biological hand. Eir face went white, crumpling into a rictus. The Matua turned, shat on the ground and stalked off into the treeline. The workers followed her.

Cheyara was fumbling in her pocket for the vial of concentrated antivenom. There was a red, puckering wound on Heron's wrist. With shaking hands she produced the vial, fumbling with the sterile seal.

'Fetch a first aid kit,' said Heron, through gritted teeth. 'You'll need to immobilise the wrist.'

She ran to the flier, reached for the first aid kit in the cockpit and darted back to Heron, who was still on eir knees, cradling eir wounded arm. She knelt, pulling back the sleeve of Heron's coat.

'Hold still.' When she'd been trained on the administration procedure, her hand hadn't been shaking. There was a sheen of sweat on Heron's forehead and red lines were spreading from the bulging, angry wound. Procedure complete, Cheyara discarded the vial.

'We have to go.' Heron said.

'But where?' Cheyara said. Heron's skin felt clammy and looked pale. She noticed a nasty red rash puckering around the wound site.

'The...emergency pickup point.'

'But that's at altitude!'

'I know.'

Heron was on eir hands and knees. Then eir limbs folded. Ey was gasping, prone on the ground. She turned em over. Heron's pulse was racing and eir face was sodden with sweat. She put em into the recovery position and fetched a pillow, insulated blanket and medical scanner from a container. She lifted eir head, placing the pillow underneath. Then she covered em with the blanket, wincing at eir laboured breathing. Activating the scanner, she moved it over eir body as instructed. The unit recorded a racing heart rate, and diagnosed ANAPHYLAXIS.

Terrific.

She grabbed an adrenaline pen from the medical kit, injecting it into Heron's lateral thigh. She squatted beside em, her eyes glued to the scanner. Eir heartrate was still too fast, and ey was gasping like a fish in air.

Dammit, Heron, I can't lose you now!

Especially not to some stupid allergic reaction. Weren't the Taiyangren supposed to have evolved beyond all that? The procedure in the medical scanner recommended two IVs, for intravenous antivenom and saline if possible. But she'd have to get Heron into the flier, first….

Oh, Jesus! She shook and her heart raced like a stallion. She forced herself to pause, using *Kapalabhati* breathing to oppose panic. The technique had a touch of familiarity, opening mental space.

Now. One problem at a time.

They'd been told to leave. This was urgent. She had no doubt that she'd be attacked if they were still here tomorrow. She still wasn't happy with the scanner readings.

An hour later, Heron was still unconscious, but eir breathing and heart rate had settled and the scanner had pronounced em stable. She set the medical scanner to issue an alarm if Heron's condition changed, then began to pack. She emptied her tent, stowing her belongings in the flier's storage compartment as the combined but weak heat of Biloko and Asali beat on her back. Fortunately, they'd long ago moved any heavy equipment back into the containers. Heron's tent was almost empty, just a sleeping bag and a small rucksack. She put eir rucksack in the flier also. She left the awning. It was too big for her to attempt to dismantle, and she wasn't going to injure herself trying.

When Cheyara was done, she told the tents to pack themselves away and they obeyed, like self-cocooning insects. She picked up the balled tents and carried them over to the flier. Then she inspected the rest of the items in the flier's storage compartment. There was only one emergency food pack stowed. That wouldn't do. She didn't fancy having to rely solely on the flier's food synthesiser, so she needed to fetch some additional food packs.

As for water: she recalled her survival training. Mountain water and snow were fairly fresh. She'd have to use sterilisation pills. She could also boil it, in an emergency.

But this is already an emergency, Cheyara thought, approaching Container 1. As she reached for the door, there was a coldness in her gut. With Freeze coming, there was no way they'd survive up there for long, at altitude. But right now there was no alternative. The flier had an automatic recall program to reach the pickup point, on which Cheyara was frankly dependent. She was a mediocre pilot at best, especially with her neural lace deactivated.

She opened the container door and there was a furtive movement at the back. She peered into the dimly-lit corner, more puzzled than afraid. Perhaps a small animal.... Then she saw a humble, peeping over a packing case.

She recognised Flora immediately. Flora issued a soft buzz of recognition and emerged from her hiding place. When she came into full light, Cheyara could see that the change had come upon the humble. An additional, weeping slit had opened at her groin and there were fully grown stingers at each wrist. She limped towards Cheyara with her hands spread in a supplicatory gesture. Cheyara saw a long, deep wound on her left leg. It looked like it was festering.

'Help me!' Flora said, 'Help me!'

INTERLUDE 3

*M*agrena requested a Taiyangren transport in the end, ignoring complaints about 'community pride.' Pragmatics was her only measure. Now the Taiyangeren had the vaccines, the transport was virus free: that was all that mattered.

From a distance Margulis resembled a sepia and white football surmounted by coating of foamy green. As the transport approached the modified exo-Kuiper belt object you could see that the green 'foam' was actually myriads of globes like green and purple grapes. Closer still and you could see that the 'grapes' were large translucent spheres, some of which contained a fluid consisting of water, nutrients and green or purple algae. Other spheres held people, equipment and furniture or manufacturing machines.

As the shark-like transport nosed between a cluster of grapes, Magrena saw two naked floating Taiyangren having sex in the middle of one sphere. She wasn't sure whether the display was for her benefit. She didn't care, much. For a time, in her youth, she'd lived in Taiyangren habitations in the solar system and had grown used to such exhibitionism.

That was almost 1,100 years ago, by the Earthian frame of reference. A gulf of time that she didn't like to think about too hard.

Someone else was watching the display. Floating outside the sphere in open space was a large, crusty brown-grey carapace with protruding armoured arms and legs. The helmet or head-end was a gold-coated hemisphere through which Magrena could see human features. The armoured Taiyangren's limbs moved slowly in the vacuum, as all-but invisible gas-jets stabilised the thick body.

The Taiyangren sculled round to watch the arrival of the craft and waved at Magrena. She waved back. This Taiyangren was a permanent resident of weightless space, visiting the pressurised chambers of Margulis as a dolphin visited the surface of the ocean to breathe.

The airlock was open. It was time for her to leave the ship.

She was greeted by a possibly young Taiyangren named Jay. Jay seemed to have modelled eir wardrobe on something out of an early twenty-first century leather and fetish catalogue, although eir feet were bare instead of booted. Like many of the younger generation, the Taiyangren had modified eir feet to be prehensile, presumably to better handle movement in low or zero g environments.

Jay escorted her down a long spiralling glowing corridor that was composed of a transparent tube supported by a highly complex silicate structure that the Taiyangren informed her was derived from the lattice skeleton of a glass sponge.

'It's typical for a Vermeulun Class settlement. The original design was intended to be a starship, you know, but proved far too slow for the exodus….'

'I remember,' Magrena said, thinking of the ill-fated ARK that had been swallowed by the fucking Zungui. They reached the end of the corridor and a door dilated. They drifted through, one after the other.

·

Magrena had been on Margulis less than four hours when Sonya pinged her. She received the message in her guest suite, which formed an eighth of one of the green spheres. The interior decor resembled the antechamber of a baroque cathedral made of translucent materials designed by architects who love ribbed and fluted glistening bright green biomechanics.

The room was dominated by a bed that was raised on a soft crystalline catafalque that at first glance seemed totally unsuited to an effectively microgravity environment. It also seemed excessive for a dumpy old woman with arthritis. Still, the bioform mattress was comfortable and the mossy cover would hold her in place while she slept.

Sonya was concise, as usual.

'We have to get them back.'

Magrena grit her teeth. The youngster really was a one-note wonder.

'I know what you're thinking. But it's not like that.' Sonya said.

'Sonya, we've only just restored this Supalite channel….'

Magrena's voice sounded adenoidal, which was not surprising because her nose was blocked and her sinuses ached. She'd spent a good portion of her adult life going to and fro from microgravity environments but she still hated them.

'Don't you care about them?' Sonya said, 'They could be injured, or dead.'

'They could. But I have confidence in them. They're resourceful. They'll be okay. We're working on the Nyuki comms satellites right now, remotely. And the Msafiri. *And the* Octavia*'s been despatched. Worst case scenario, we pick them up in fifty days.'*

'If they're still alive!'

'Sometimes you just have to roll the dice.'

'You'd know all about that, wouldn't you?' Sonya said.

Magrena cut the connection.

Idealists were always tiresome. And idealism was a common affliction of the young. Like measles—used to be.

Magrena shoved herself off the edge of the catafalque and drifted towards the edge of the room, avoiding collision by stretching out her hand. The wall gave a little under her palm. It felt slightly rubbery, the algae-rich soup that filled the cavity between its transparent layers forming swirling patterns that radiated from her spread fingers. This close the brightest stars shone through the green murk.

She spun, focusing her gaze on the catafalque. She felt nauseous from the microgravity and wondered once more how the Taiyang-ren coped. Of course, from the outset they had been specially and deliberately modified for this sort of environment. A third and forth generation Taiyangren's bones and cardiovascular system were self-maintaining and did not degenerate after a lifetime in a microgravity environment.

They were radiation-hardy, too, almost invulnerable to cosmic-ray induced cancers—although that was one adaptation the relatively conservative Abodans had also been forced to adopt. Gene-editing for hard radiation environments was not an option out here. It was a necessity.

A deep, sonorous bell began to toll. Magrena paddled uselessly in mid-air, cursing her own ineptitude. She grabbed a wall-protrusion and shuttled herself towards the door, which irised open.

Jay was waiting outside. She hoped ey hadn't been outside her room all this time. The tolling bell was louder in the tubular corridor. Jay said nothing but began using regular wall protrusions to move swiftly down the curving tube. Magrena followed, a little jealous of the Taiyangren's supple movements and prehensile feet. Although she was a little too conservative to try such a radical modification, she could see why it was practical on Margulis.

They entered a larger chamber that was a fully transparent hemisphere bathed in diffuse golden light. Fish swam in random directions in the walls amongst fronds of kelp. The space was host to about a dozen floating Taiyangren, most of whom wore clothes. One or two talked quietly together, but the majority remained silent. *Gestures and nods indicated that they were conversing via their Cloud.*

The room was dominated by a transparent, open, roughly globular frame structure with embedded biomorph chairs that matched the soft crystal decor of the hemispherical room. Magrena found a seat and perched awkwardly. She directed her attention to the Taiyangren person who sat in the opposite chair. Their eyes locked and the Taiyangren nodded. Corncrake E Shrew's hair was swept back and immaculate, somehow staying in place even in microgravity. Ey was clad in a plain mauve tunic.

Magrena smiled, raising her eyebrows. Corncrake held up crossed fingers.

'Second time lucky,' *Magrena said, holding up two sets of crossed fingers.*

'Third time. Michael and Raphael were both trashed, remember.'

Corncrake looked only very slightly older than when they'd first met on Earth, all those centuries ago. Then, ey would have been in eir early thirties. By a simple act of kindness, Corncrake had saved her from the Zungui. Would ey be able to save her again?

Perhaps.

If there was any single person who could pull this off, it was Corncrake.

By now, the other Taiyangren had taken their places.

'You already know,' *Corncrake said, speaking aloud for Magrena's benefit,* 'that Gabriel approached a Zungui node twenty hours ago. We've been monitoring their functions via Supalite all the way.'

'Is that safe?' *Magrena said, and Corncrake shrugged.*

'The Zungui have assured Gabriel that the vaccines work. And the informational scotoma's been removed from our Supalite network, so….'

Magrena waved crossed fingers.

'Exactly,' *Corncrake said.* 'Now, it took several hours to establish contact. It seems that the Zungui have upgraded their machine languages.

Unfortunately, the languages we had on file were half a century or so out of date. They generously sent Gabriel an update and we were away.'

Corncrake activated a projection that materialised in the air in the centre of the seating structure. The projection showed a livestream from the probe in system NGS 554121, three light years away and transmitted via a hopefully clean Supalite channel. There wasn't much to see: a sprinkling of stars in space and the convoluted, bulging edge of the Zungui structure to which the probe was docked. No ignorant observer would have guessed from the image that the fate of two sentient species would be determined by the outcome of the docking.

Corncrake gestured and a large, digital stopwatch materialised in the top left of the image. The stopwatch, which was counting up, read 15:34:26.

'That's how long they've been negotiating,' Ey said.

'Are you sure it's wise, leaving the diplomacy to a machine?' Magrena said.

'Good question. We did consider patching in a comms channel so we could negotiate ourselves, but unfortunately it seems that Zungui cognitive functions now vastly outstrip our own.'

'What, even with your enhancements?' Magrena said.

'Even with our enhancements. We're cyborgs but our thinking is still rooted in the biology of our brains. I can tell you from personal experience that souping up cognitive functions has…costs. Unless the Zungui decide to construct an emissary, the only option is to let Gabriel do our negotiating for us.'

'So we can do nothing?'

'There's a drink synthesiser over there.'

Magrena risked leaving her seat to get a coffee. Jay helped, making her feel even more like a little old lady. She was joined by others who were probably also anxious for distraction. Still, their prevailing silence unnerved her. For a time, she gazed at the fish in the concave wall, conscious of the active livestream behind her. The coffee, when it came, was the best she'd ever tasted.

Later, she gripped a soft crystal protuberance next to Corncrake, who remained enthroned in eir biomorph chair. The stopwatch accumulated minutes.

'It's good to see you again, Magrena. You should….'

'…visit us more often.'

'As you say….'

Magrena saw a Taiyangren floating in midair in a semi-foetal position with eir head in eir hands. The Taiyangren was sobbing. Tears floated in droplets around eir head.

'It's been hard for everyone,' Corncrake said, following her gaze.

'Yes. The screw keeps turning, doesn't it?'

'It never stops. That's the universe for you.'

'You talk as if it's already too late.'

'In a sense, it was too late the moment the Zungui decided to eat the universe….'

The sonorous bell tolled again. There was immediate silence as the gaze of every person in the room was riveted to the hologram. The livestream showed wheeling stars and then a brief glimpse of a vast, biotech landscape of elaborate, glowing, arboreal, spiderweb structures. The complex surface was retreating behind the probe, revealing quasi-metallic, intricate, arterial, fractal patterns that reflected the light of their distant, red sun.

Magrena's heart leapt into overdrive. The negotiations must have ended. This was confirmed a moment later when Gabriel began to speak. She realised that she was holding Corncrake's hand. She felt almost dizzy with fright, but helpless to do anything but listen as the probe intoned their fate.

The deep bell kept ringing.

IV ASCENT

24TH MARCH A.Y. 88

MISSION ELAPSED TIME: 578 days.
LOCATION: NORTHERN SUBCONTINENT 2, NYUKI.
HUMBLE TERRITORY.

They sat in the flier with the canopy down. Cheyara was in the pilot's seat with Flora opposite, in the co-pilot's position. The display before them showed the Emergency Flight Path Menu. Cheyara had only to tap the red square and the flier would take off, following a programmed course to the pickup point. She was not yet ready to execute.

Flora's leg wound was bound and she was sucking on a

bottle filled with liquid 'sugar.' Some time ago, Heron had shown Cheyara how to program the onboard synthesiser to produce food with a biochemistry suited for humbles. The application had seemed pointless at the time.

Heron was behind them, strapped into a reclining back seat. The medical scanner lay on the adjacent seat, beeping in time to Heron's heartbeat. There was an IV push in the back of eir hand that was attached to a saline drip, and a second that administered hydrocortisone. Cheyara had also spent some time putting in a catheter.

Despite her leg wound, Flora had helped Cheyara lift Heron into the flier. An unconscious Heron was heavy as a sack of lead and at first Cheyara had struggled alone. Flora had watched for about five seconds before lending a hand. Cheyara was grateful: the humble had a wiry strength despite her childlike size, one of the gifts of Matuahood. It would have taken far longer without Flora, with the additional risk of further injuring Heron.

After they got Heron to the seat, Flora had watched as Cheyara followed the spoken instructions of the medical scanner. Cheyara suspected that Flora would be able to mimic the procedures pretty closely if required.

Now Flora was speaking, her words a jumble of Earthian and Humble. Excited, her normal fluency was gone. Cheyara activated the translator on a tablet, watching word after word materialise in large, blocky letters on the screen.

'Slowly, Flora, Slowly.'

Flora slowed, a little.

FOOD WALK.

The translator attempted.

WE WERE ON FOOD WALK.

'Say it again,' Cheyara said, then repeated herself in a clumsy imitation of the humble language. Dammit, she'd always been crap at that! Flora was probably hearing gibberish!

But Flora's head bobbed, and she repeated the string of words.

FORAGING TRIP.

I SMELT OLD ON THEM.

I KNEW I WAS DIFFERENT.

Cheyara listened, only half understanding, at first. It helped that Flora had slowed down and was speaking more persistently in Earthian. Later, Cheyara would edit a more polished transcription, which would become part of their shared history.

But that was in the future.

And this was now.

.

Flora had been on a foraging trip when ey had felt the change come upon her. That day the suns were bright and the morning was warm. It was one of the last settled days of the dying season.

There were four of them in total, each carrying a wicker basket. Early on, Flora overtook eir siblings, finding emself a hundred or more paces ahead along the forest trail. Eir siblings walked slowly, often pausing for a rest, sitting down or leaning against tree trunks. Flora watched them from a distance, listening to their halting breath and low humming talk.

When they finally caught up, Flora smelt their old age, sour scents that seemed somehow more indelible than their wrinkled, sagging faces. Witnessing the decrepitude of her companions, Flora felt no sorrow, only a vague disquiet. Perhaps she sensed that eir fate might have already diverged from theirs.

The party arrived at a grove of giant trees that produced succulent gourd-like fruit with thick skins and rich, sweet flesh. Collecting the gourds was laborious. Flora climbed high into the branches and sawed the tough stalk of a single large fruit with a flint knife. Once the fruit was cut free, ey descended to the lower branch where one of eir companions was waiting. The second worker received the fruit and passed it to one of the two humbles who waited on the ground.

Flora was climbing along a high limb when ey felt a tingle at eir groin and a dull, mild ache in her bowels. The tingling spread throughout her body, arresting her progress along the limb. The wave of sensation reached her head and the world spun about her. She almost fell but hugged the tree limb and squeezed her eyes shut. Exciting and terrifying thoughts rocketed through her brain.

Her companions were calling to her but she barely heard. Eventually the sensations subsided and she was able to descend with a fruit. She knew that once the changes became visible, she would become Matua's enemy. She saw this clearly in her mind. There was only one solution available to her.

Her gaze fell on her companions. The two on the ground were talking to the humble who was immediately below her. The one in the tree was feeling tired, and wanted to come down. The others sat on the ground, beside half-full baskets. Their sibling was already climbing down the main trunk, panting heavily. Flora waited until ey reached the bottom before following.

Once on the ground, her fellow workers did not even glance in her direction. They kept talking amongst themselves. It was as if she did not exist. Perhaps they subliminally sensed the change within her. Perhaps not. Flora sat apart from them, waiting for her moment. She was ready to leave.

For some time she'd been avoiding the House, except for last thing at night, or for brief visits to deposit food. With the other foragers, she'd spent many hours and days trekking to the periphery of their territory. So she knew where the good foraging was, and would survive by staying as far from the House as possible. But there was a danger. If she was not careful, the Matua would sense her location, even if she ran away.

Here Flora used a humble word that translated as *together, unified, bond, kin* and, confusingly, *all*. She supplemented this with another word that meant, depending on context, *near, no-place, location*. Cheyara thought of the times when the hatchery workers had seemed to anticipate the arrival of a forager. She also thought of the day when she'd confronted the vespon, and how Flora and the others had been at the Basecamp when the flier had arrived. There were other times, too, when the humbles had seemed to know things that they really shouldn't.

Unified, bond, no-place, location?

Flora had one ability that she'd never discussed with anyone. Until then it had seemed useless. On one of her first foraging trips, way back in spring, she'd become lost. The young Flora had wandered for hours before chancing upon a trail that she knew. During that time, she'd experienced a yawning, overpowering, horrifying sense of isolation. That terror had somehow severed her invisible link with the collective. Later, by chance, she discovered that she could cut herself off at will. All she had to do was remember, vividly, how it had felt when she was alone. So she cut the link inside—'made the un-bond'—then fled from the grove when none of them was looking.

The first short night she built a temporary nest up in a tree. In the nest she would be safe from the predators that patrolled the forest in full darkness. But on her first night alone, she discovered that survival was more than a matter of food and shelter. No longer connected to the whole, she felt as if an arm had been severed. Towards dawn she experienced a profound desolation that she'd never suspected was possible. Her limbs felt heavy and her head throbbed. She felt a coldness in her gut.

A part of her wanted to end the pain. Perhaps she would seek out a vespon and allow herself to be eaten. Surely that would be preferable to permanent exile.

Flora stopped speaking.

'I felt…I cannot say the word….' She was switching again to her own language, pronouncing a single phrase which the AI translated as '*no longer part of the [social] body.*' This was the humble word for *corpse*. She'd become one of the walking dead.

The next morning she descended from the tree in a numb state and almost fell prey to a pack of googers. In ordinary times, she would have evaded them with ease, but they gave chase through the forest. She only escaped by fording a river and climbing another tree.

Afterwards, with hunger jabbing in her gut, she returned to the grove where they'd foraged for the gourd-fruit. The trampled ground, broken twigs and vestigial scents of her siblings were like ghosts of her old life. She hesitated, looking down the trail that led, eventually, to the House. Then she climbed up the tree. Most of the fruit had been harvested, but there was one large one left at the extremity of an upper limb. The limb sagged as she approached the fruit. At arm's length, she began cutting the stalk with a flint knife she'd found abandoned at the base of the tree. The fruit fell to the ground with a thud.

She descended the tree and found half the fruit flattened

and badly bruised. She cut the unbruised half open with the flint knife and guzzled the sweet flesh. Then she stood and looked down the trail again. She felt a little stronger, but the magnetic pull of family was almost irresistible. Surely things had not really changed that much. Surely things would be...normal.

Unified, bond, kin.

She began to wander back along the trail in the direction of the House. Perhaps it was from instinct, perhaps it was from a need to heal the pain of being alone.

Unified, bond, kin.

On the way she encountered two males, sitting languidly against trees. One hummed an invitation to her, but she ran away. For the first time she felt an attraction, but it was an urge that she was not yet ready to indulge.

She approached the House downwind, sniffing the air. She expected familiar, comforting scents, but there was something else. This odour popped the bubble of her illusions, prompting withdrawal.

She scented humble blood.

·

Days and nights passed and Flora survived on the outer perimeter of the House territory. Fruit, berries and edible nuts were getting hard to find, but Flora knew where to look. She could eat roots, fungus, insects and even small animals if necessary. At the end of each day-cycle she slept in a different tree, which was the best way to avoid the attention of predators. Over time, the aching sense of loss and loneliness faded and she felt almost at one with the dying forest.

Her body was still changing. These changes were

signalled by further aches in her limbs and belly and groin. One day she woke up with a strong need that overwhelmed everything else. With a new sense of urgency, she sniffed the air, soon locating the desired scent.

The male lolled beneath a tree a safe distance from the House. She approached him in a semi-trance. When they coupled, it was a strange mixture of pleasure and pain. Then the moment of impregnation came and she knew that she was more than a rogue. She was now a Matua. Her body was now robust enough to survive hibernation and the long cold. In the Spring, a time aeons distant, she might found a new House of her own.

Afterwards, she pushed him away. He fell against the trunk of the tree and sank, content to the ground. He would soon die. It was the way of things.

At that moment, she felt the direct contact of another mind. A powerful, old and very familiar mind. For a moment, the two minds shared *everything*.

It was Matua, of course.

Flora felt her Matua's crippling fear. She saw her terror of lost control and horror of encroaching oblivion. Flora saw that she lashed out because of her pain.

The sharing went both ways. Flora felt Matua's dawning consciousness of her rival. Matua now knew exactly what she'd done. She felt her aged parent's furious, murderous rage and knew that she was in mortal danger. But she was also powerful. She severed the link.

·

They would be after her now. Her only choice was to flee to the mountains. But it was too early. Before she went, Flora would need to feed to store fat so that her body could endure the arduous journey and six-year sleep. Here, the juvenile Matuas had the advantage. They could feed on the honey stores at the House, making the final trek only when replete. The honey stores were a major reason why in normal times, a rogue would have to kill their Matua. Often it was the only way to gain access to those stores.

Outside, food sources remained scarce. She revisited all the prime foraging sites, finding them mostly barren. So she had to travel further to find food, which used yet more precious energy and fat. The days and nights were growing colder. This meant that she needed even more food to stay warm at night.

One night she saw a roving patrol composed of her siblings corner two demi-rogues who were fleeing to the mountains. She listened to the hums of distress and fear and the stinging silence afterwards. She smelt more fresh blood before slipping away.

They would not catch her like that. They would *never* catch her like that.

Too soon, her silent promise was broken. Flora encountered a patrol at a foraging site. She retreated into the bushes as fast as she could.

Too late. One face was turned in her direction. Their eyes met, and they both hesitated. Flora smelt her sibling's weakness and age. Then she sensed eir hatred. Ey raised eir arm and pitched a rock, which hit her thigh.

She ignored the searing pain and fled to the river, wading as far upstream as she could. This was risky. Predatory eels had scented the dripping blood and were circling. One approached and nipped her leg. She pulled herself out of the river and lay gasping on the bank, then hid deep in the rotting autumn underbrush.

She knew she'd been lucky. If the worker had been

younger, eir aim would have been surer. She was fairly sure eir target had been Flora's head.

She heard the voices of other humbles in the forest, and her hearts beat faster, her lung-books pulsing until they ached. Eventually, the voices faded and she knew that she'd evaded them. Biloko and Asali, close in the sky, would still be above the horizon for some time. She must hide.

By nightfall her leg became stiff and immobile and she knew that unless she could heal she would not have the stamina or speed to get to the mountains. She convulsed with uncontrollable shivers. Her body was so weak that she did not have the strength even to climb a tree. Only good fortune would prevent her from being discovered and eaten that night.

She was dozing when a dream-image popped into her consciousness. The image brought her to full wakefulness and she pulled herself to her feet. She was still shivering and her extremities were numb. It was obvious what she should do. She was surprised that she'd not thought of it before. This season, like the last, the order of the world had changed. She had an option that had not ever existed on her world before.

There were still a couple of hours of darkness left, and this was an unnatural time for humbles. But she realised that was an advantage. They would not search again until dawn.

The dream-image had told her exactly where to go.

·

'I remembered this flitter,' Flora said, gesturing about her. 'I remembered that you helped us, before. I want you to help me.'

'How?'

'You must fly me away, to the mountains. I must escape Matua.'

Cheyara closed eir eyes.

'It's not that easy,' Cheyara said. She could only bend the contact protocols so far. They might be cut off, but her actions were still being recorded.

'I know your life is different from ours,' Flora said. 'I know that your family has told you not to interfere. But you are here. You have changed us already.'

Something hit the windscreen, bouncing off. Cheyara twisted in her seat. Three humbles stood below. Two were armed with stone axes and the third had a rock in eir hand.

Cheyara strapped herself in, and Flora followed suit, imitating her without a fumble. Cheyara reached for the red square on the display and hesitated.

Was this right?

Then Flora jabbed the square.

The engine fired as the rock struck the windscreen. The whine of the engines rose and Cheyara peeped at their persecutors. One had raised eir axe and looked as if they were about to thrust it in a rotor blade. A vein pulsed in Cheyara's temple.

The flier lurched off the ground, ascending over the top of the canopy. The forest below was a patchwork of mouldy, moist browns, yellows and greys. Most of the ground cover had rotted, and patches of grey earth were visible. Cheyara could see the nearer trails and the large clearing to the east where the House lay.

The flier wheeled, pitching at an angle that always made Cheyara feel a little dizzy. She glanced back. Heron's head was lolling, but there was nothing she could do. She really should have secured em better.

They climbed to the thick cloud layer, the flier shuddering from turbulence. Flora remained silent throughout the ascent. They burst through into sunlight, with Biloko and Asali shining blended light on a baroque cloudscape. Flora emitted a hum of delight.

.

The emergency pickup point was on a small plateau at the edge of the treeline in the mountains. The trees here were smaller, with thick waxy leaves. Patches of snow on the ground were tinged red-gold in the combined light of the twin suns.

The flier landed, the rotors slowing to a halt. Then there was nothing but the sound of their breathing, the wind and the quiet beeping of the medical scanner.

'I need to feed,' Flora said and Cheyara nodded. She pushed the button on the food synthesiser which dispensed another bottle of alien, liquid sugar. Flora grabbed it and sucked hard. The bottle was soon empty.

'More.'

In the end, she had two more. Then she asked to be let out.

They opened the canopy and Flora clambered down the short ladder to the snow. Cheyara followed, immediately wishing she'd pulled on a jacket. Her breath was clouding and an icy chill blew from the mountains.

There was a small shuttle-placed container parked on the edge of the little plateau, serving as an emergency supply station. Cheyara had forgotten its existence in her panic. Trudging through snow, she opened the door and inspected the equipment within. She found a food synthesiser and a surgical unit, neither of which responded to repeated jabs of the 'on' switch. The Zungui viruses had obviously been at work here also. Some smaller bits of equipment were okay—she found a working medical scanner and also a water filtration unit. There were additional food packs and medical supplies, bedding, tents and a fairly pathetic emergency shelter. She closed the door of the container, wincing at the windchill.

Flora was scanning jagged peaks and sniffing the air. The terminal end of a large glacier was visible beyond the descending arête that marked the western edge of the plateau. The level ground on which they stood ended in a cirque and was evidence that Nyuki was currently enjoying a period of comparative warmth, geologically speaking. Cheyara knew enough geology to interpret the surrounding features as evidence of even more extensive glaciation in the past. Perhaps 5,000 years previously, the cirque would have been under ice.

'This is a good place,' Flora said.

27TH MARCH A.Y. 88

MISSION ELAPSED TIME: 581 days.
LOCATION: NORTHERN SUBCONTINENT 2, NYUKI.
EMERGENCY PICKUP POINT AT ALTITUDE.

R ed day and Cheyara, insomniac, was woken by Biloko after an all too brief period of darkness. She sat stiff-necked in the pilot's seat of the flier. Her bottom had gone to sleep. She rubbed her eyes, twisting to see in the back.

Drool was hanging off Heron's gaunt chin. She scrambled into the adjacent back seat, grabbed a wipe and cleaned the drool away. Then she inspected the medical scanner, which was advising a fresh dose of hydrocortisone. There were fresh pouches in the emergency supply station, which meant cracking the canopy and letting the cold air in. She scrambled out, briefly scanning the little plateau for Flora. She was nowhere to be seen, but then Cheyara spied a line of footprints heading south. South: that was downhill. No doubt she was looking for more food.

Once she'd set up the hydrocortisone pouch, she saw that the scanner was also reminding her to administer the daily dose of anticoagulant to Heron's abdomen. This was not possible because the medical supplies she'd brought lacked anticoagulant. Nor had she found any in the station. She'd checked twice three days before. Also advised was the fitting of a nasogastric tube for feeding, which she also lacked. Anyway, the fitting procedure was beyond her current medical skillset. Afterwards, she turned Heron, who lay in an awkward position on eir side while she checked for pressure sores.

And that was all that she could do.

The medical scanner was still offering no explanation for Heron's continuing state of unconsciousness. The venom had triggered a severe allergic reaction, but the hydrocortisone had helped reduce systemic inflammation and eir autonomic nervous system hadn't been too badly affected. Breathing, heart rate, blood pressure, kidney filtration all registered as nominal. Eir's temperature was also stable. And yet ey was still unconscious. It was baffling.

She spent a little time scouring Heron's medical records, looking for any clue about eir condition. Date of Birth: sixth of September 2081, Common Era. So from an Earthian frame of reference, Heron was 1,106 years old. Actually minus the thirteen years or so relativistic cryosleep time, Heron was one hundred and fourteen years old and looking very good on it. Ey was first-generation Taiyangren with a genome that according to the record had been edited in the laboratories of the Tsan Yuk Teaching Hospital in Hong Kong. Eir's fertilised embryo had subsequently been frozen for passage to 16 Psyche in Sol's Asteroid belt. Egg donor: 'Susie Chen,' which Cheyara strongly suspected to be a pseudonym. According to the record, 'Susie Chen's' career was Genetic Engineer. No other parents were named.

Anyway, a birth date of 2081. That would mean that Heron wasn't technically born a Taiyangren. She happened to know that the designation wasn't affirmed until 2092, the year of their independence declaration and fifteen years after the Zungui had initiated their master plan. So Heron had grown up in the most tumultuous, and in some ways terminal, period of human history.

One hundred and fourteen. A long life, longer than many Earthians, or Abodans, for that matter, had enjoyed. And the medical record told her some of it. Various phases of somatic interface implantation from the age of five onwards. A broken arm in March 2099 at the age of seventeen. Full neural lace fitted eight months later, at eighteen. Two broken ribs in 2107, a year before the exodus. A thirteen—or nine hundred and ninety two—year gap of cold sleep. Twelve longevity therapy treatments since their arrival at Asali. Modification of the liver and kidneys. New somatic interfaces grown *in situ* from 3104 Common Era, the year before the Asali Consilience Settlement. Addition of the bionic hand in 3110. More somatic interfaces added in 3140 and 3144 (or Abode Year 40 and 44).

Heron, in short, was walking history. And despite their time together, ey'd disclosed almost none of it.

And if they didn't get help soon, ey might well starve to death while still unconscious. What a shitty end to a long life. But she supposed that all deaths were.

.

Later, Cheyara squatted before the line of footprints that led downhill, off the little plateau that was now her place of exile. The footprints led in the direction of the low mountain forest where there was no doubt passable foraging. Cheyara was wearing a down coat, which the cold wind penetrated. There were goosebumps on her skin. The sky was only lightly clouded and stained pink by Biloko. The dark blue sky was visible in patches beyond. The view of the Mountains was sharp. Her breath puffed in clouds.

She straightened up, hoping that Flora knew what she was doing. She daren't venture too far from the flier: she had to stay close to Heron. She also couldn't risk injury. A broken ankle, in this situation, could mean the difference between life and death.

The air certainly felt colder today, with the wind moaning down the arête. She walked in a slow circle, marking out a wide O in the snow. Later, she started stamping, upping her circulation to combat the stiffness in her muscles.

From only a little distance, the flier looked tiny and vulnerable against a background of cyclopean, snow-shrouded rock. Right now it was their refuge, their single hope for survival. Fortunately, it was currently in good shape. The surface was covered in photovoltaics, which could in theory supply nominal power even with midwinter levels of insolation. The primary source, however, was the fusion engine, which had sufficient fuel for another twenty years, at least. The problem was the secondary systems. The flier had not been designed to weather a winter. She'd run a simulation and there was a high probability of breakdowns over six years of cold. They'd be better off returning to Basecamp, where there was a shelter and the supplies in the container.

But who was she kidding? It wouldn't be 'we.' It would be her. Alone. In that scenario, Heron would be dead and Flora would be long gone, hibernating deep in the mountains. She would be utterly solitary. And it was a decision that might have to be made within a short run of *days*.

The cloud-haze broke, revealing Biloko like a baleful eye gazing down upon her. In that moment, the bloated red star seemed like a savage god, a witness to the termination of her too-brief life. Heron was one hundred and fourteen. She was twenty-seven.

It wasn't fair.

It just wasn't fair!

She felt as if she'd barely touched life. For a moment, she felt more frustrated and pissed off than frightened. There was so much she'd wanted to do. So much that she'd wanted to see. So many people she'd wanted to love.

She'd faced death several times on this expedition. She'd endured smaller hazards innumerable times. But this was the first time that she'd felt an icy, clammy touch of despair.

29TH MARCH A.Y. 88

MISSION ELAPSED TIME: 583 days.
LOCATION: NORTHERN SUBCONTINENT 2. NYUKI.
EMERGENCY PICKUP POINT AT ALTITUDE.

A new, crackling voice woke her. Pre-dawn on day six, with Biloko and Asali drifting together. Almost a heat day, but no longer worthy of the name. She opened her eyes and saw breath-steam on the transparent canopy ten centimetres from her face. Then she heard a tinny voice. She lifted her head and rubbed her neck. Heron was still unconscious, behind her, the medical scanner beeping out the rhythm of his life.

She picked up the mobile transceiver from where it was lying on the co-pilot's seat and listened. There was one message, repeated over and over.

COMMS SATELLITE HAS BEEN RESTORED. PLEASE ACCESS FLIER COMMS DISPLAY.

She opened a notification on the display over the dashboard. It confirmed that radio-communications had been restored. They were expecting the Supalite to be ready later in the day. She stared at the notification, numb to its implications. After more than half a year, the world of Abode seemed remote and unreal.

'The *Msafiri*,' she said to herself, 'What about the *Msafiri*?'

The second and third paragraphs of the notification answered that question. They were running software diagnostics currently, and had already diverted the *Octavia* in case of emergency.

The final paragraph:

We received your emergency broadcast. A medical advisor will be in touch shortly.

But how 'shortly?' Heron was stable but needed immediate expert attention. She'd already exhausted the medical scanner's relevant instructional videos. And without a nasogastric tube, ey was in danger of starvation.

Cheyara suddenly felt claustrophobic. She opened the flier's canopy and wandered over to the snow. Flora was standing on boulders, looking down at the glacier.

The cold wind was icy, but refreshed Cheyara. It was all too much to take in. Their isolation had produced a feeling of acute withdrawal, and strangely a part of her dreaded the resumption of human contact. But it was necessary.

.

As promised, the Supalite was restored towards the end of the day. The 'medical advisor' was in contact first: a Taiyangren. By then she'd sent them the scanner's recordings of the medical history of the sting and subsequent complications.

'Taiyangren have deep brain implants, with emergency programming,' the advisor told her, 'After the anaphylaxis, an implant near eir brain's reticular activation system turned on, keeping em in an unconscious state. It's a form of defence.'

'How come the implant never switched em back on?' Cheyara said.

The Taiyangren winced.

'Unfortunately, Heron's systems were attacked by a Zungui virus some time ago. It was obviously never fully purged from eir bionic systems.'

'Ey never told me.'

'Ey probably didn't want to worry you. But with the Supalite activated, Heron's linked to our Cloud again and I can reset the implant. Ey should wake in the next few minutes.'

Chayara didn't dare move until Heron's eyes opened. Ey was slow to answer the questions the medical scanner asked, assessing cognitive function. Afterwards, ey looked at Cheyara.

'So we made it.' Cheyara nodded.

Heron sipped some water and then accepted a bottle of food concentrate from Cheyara, which ey almost dropped. Cheyara held the nipple up to eir mouth.

'I'm going to need to move,' ey said, afterwards.

Removing the IV, Cheyara helped unfasten the webbing that had bound eir to the seat. At first, Heron performed joint mobilisation exercises in the confined space of the cockpit. Then ey had some more liquid food concentrate. Later they opened the canopy and she helped Heron down the short ladder to the snow. It was a slow process, with Heron repeatedly stumbling on the steps.

Heron paced small, slow circles in the snow. By the end of each circuit, eir step was a little more vigorous. Fortunately ey hadn't been unconscious for long enough for eir muscles to seriously atrophy. Taiyangren physiology, adapted to microgravity, was anyway resistant to such degeneration.

Flora was watching them from across the site. Heron nodded at the humble.

'I guess you can fill me in later.'

'Along with the rest of humanity.'

'I'm sure you did the right thing.'

'It wasn't entirely my decision.'

Heron smiled.

'Good,' Ey said.

.

Later, back in the flier. Two committee members appeared on the shared flier display: Agara and Ahmed.

'We got your report....' Agara said.

'And we're glad you're okay,' Ahmed said. Cheyara didn't dare ask where Magrena and Sonya were.

The topic of Flora didn't come up in the meeting, but they had to be aware of the situation. Towards the end of the dialogue, Cheyara noticed the humble standing outside in the snow, watching the flier. She wondered how much the humble understood. More than they'd anticipated, she was sure.

As the day unfolded, the details of their situation became clearer. The *Msafiri* was fully functional and a shuttle could be dispatched within a few days. And they were both surprised when Agara told them that the vaccine had been of Zungui origin.

'The first probe—Michael—flew through a cloud of industrial tailings. It seems the cloud was partly composed of discarded dark matter/energy information-structures. Michael's systems were corrupted pretty fast and the damage spread into the Supalite network. They called it an informational scotoma.'

'What's that?'

Agara shrugged.

'Anyway it was an accident.'

At this point, Agara hesitated.

'There's something else. But Magrena wanted to tell you.'

.

Magrena pinged her mid-evening, when snow had begun to fall again. It was a novelty to see the notification appear in her visual field, after all this time depending on tablets. The elder was on board a Taiyangren transport, *en route* for Abode 1. The communication was still audio only.

'I heard what happened,' she said, 'I hope certain persons haven't been giving you a hard time.'

'Haven't heard from them. How are the Taiyangren?'

'In recovery, like the rest of us. But there's something else. We're making it public very soon, but I thought you two should know first. It's about the Zungui. We…or rather the Taiyangren were able to negotiate, via another probe.'

'Oh really?'

Cheyara's heart was beating faster.

'Yes. We got an outcome. The colonisation wavefront was on its way, as we suspected, but for now they've agreed to deactivate any seed replicators that enter the Asali system….'

'For now…?'

'Yes,' Magrena said. 'They've given us five hundred years.'

A green aurora danced over the mountaintops. A cold wind moaned outside, sending old snow pattering onto the flier's awning. Her heart was throbbing in her ears.

Cheyara burst into tears.

30TH MARCH A.Y. 88

MISSION ELAPSED TIME: 584 days.
LOCATION: NORTHERN SUBCONTINENT 2. NYUKI.
EMERGENCY PICKUP POINT AT ALTITUDE.

The next morning, she was able to have a conversation with her brother and sister. There was interference from Biloko, so it was still audio only. Occasionally, the channel crackled. At first she spoke to Leyon, who was his usual placid self. Then Ayanna and she spoke. The first thing that Ayanna did was tell her about Sonya.

'She left the committee.'

'How do you know?'

'Well, Ahmed came around the house. He wanted to talk to me. He was feeling guilty about what they'd done to you, you know, on that day....'

Cheyara recalled the vote, nine months previously. Like their current conversation, it seemed part of another life.

'He abstained, didn't he?'

'Yes. And when Sonya found out, she went ape. She said their pledge had been broken.'

'Did he say why he'd changed his mind?'

'Well, he still disagreed with the Expedition. He still thought it was a mistake. But he'd watched you, and the humbles. He said he understand why you'd volunteered to do it. He respected you. So he abstained. Then when all the virus shit came down he felt guilty. He thought he'd condemned you and Heron to death.'

'So he came to you.'

'Yes. I guess he couldn't apologise to you.'

'No, I guess he couldn't.'

Later, they talked of Ayanna's life. It was hard to tell, with audio only, but she sounded more alive than she had for many years.

'Every morning,' Ayanna said, 'I pray in the church. Several of us do.'

'What for?'

A pause. Then, hesitant:

'Maybe we're giving thanks.'

'For what?'

'Time.'

.

And yet, there was also a shadow. All that they'd done was to kick the can down the road. They'd received a stay of execution, marking the lifespan of their settlement but hopefully not their community. Their residence in the Asali system would last five hundred years. Once that time was up, they'd have to pile into starships and flee once again. The humbles, too, might still have to become fellow refugees.

This new exodus was now a challenge for future generations and not their own. So the Abodans were repeating a strategy that had been common practice on the Earth, a default response to the climate breakdown and mass extinction that had anticipated the Zungui's final act. The problem was that the can could only be kicked so far.

Still, it was the best outcome that could be expected in the circumstances. After the meeting with her family had ended, she watched the videos that in future years would become key documents in their unfolding history. She saw Magrena clutching the hand of Corncrake E Shrew and her never-very-professional composure breaking as the probe announced the result.

Cheyara searched for Flora, but she was nowhere to be seen.

'We have to tell her,' she said to Heron, who was fiddling with the innards of their emergency food synthesiser.

'Of course.'

'I thought you'd say that it was against the Contact Protocols.'

'Technically,' Heron said, 'But this is a shared danger, isn't it?'

Later she was sitting on a boulder a few metres from the flier when she saw Flora descending the boulders of the arête. She marvelled at the humble's sure-footedness: Magrena would no doubt have made allusions to a mountain goat. Then Flora was trudging through snow towards her, breath puffing from her breathing spiracles. The membranes that half-covered her eyes in the summer, protection from bright sunlight, were fully withdrawn.

'You are frightened.' The humble said.

'Not exactly. But there is a great danger ahead for my people. For yours also.'

The ensuing conversation was a struggle, as anticipated. She was still uncertain how much Flora really understood about their origins, and their power. More fundamentally, there were context issues. The humbles had no frame of reference for superior beings, mythic or literal, certainly not ones with effectively supernatural powers.

'The Zungui are like humans but stronger,' she said, 'They want us to...change so that we can be like them. But if we did that then everything we are would be destroyed.'

'Why do they want this?'

'They believe they need to.'

'But why?'

Cheyara shook her head in frustration.

'They just *do*. Like… like the vespon needs to kill. They need to…eat everyone who isn't like them.'

Flora was staring at her.

'What?'

'This is why you're here, isn't it? You wanted to protect us.'

Cheyara nodded, thinking of the wooden object that sat in the bottom of her luggage.

'But I'm afraid that we can't. I'm afraid that we failed. I'm afraid that we hurt you.' she said.

'These Zungui are like the cold,' Flora said. 'When the cold comes, everything dies that does not sleep.'

'Yes, exactly. But Flora, this will not be for many summers, yet. It is a problem for the future. For your descendants.'

'But it still hurts today.'

'Yes.'

Flora touched the top of her gloved hand.

'Then you must learn how to sleep, before the cold comes. Perhaps we could teach you how.'

7TH APRIL A.Y. 88

MISSION ELAPSED TIME: 590 days.
LOCATION: NORTHERN SUBCONTINENT 2. NYUKI.
EMERGENCY PICKUP POINT AT ALTITUDE.

Six days before departure, Flora descended into the hanging valley sloping down from the plateau to forage. Cheyara went with her. At first she'd been reluctant to leave Heron, but ey had shooed her on.

'I'm fine,' Ey had said. 'Go. But be careful.'

'Always!'

The mountain ecosystem was entirely different from the humble's forest. There were needle trees that were only just taller than Cheyara and smaller, hardy bushes with thick, waxy leaves and black berries. Flora gathered some of the berries in a bag she'd borrowed from the flier. She said the berries must be ground before eating.

The trees had already secreted a thick layer of cryobark, as Freeze began earlier at altitude. They were also slowly shedding leaves. Fertilised seeds had been expelled from the open cones that littered the ground. Soon the whole forest would enter a state of hibernation.

Later, they descended further and found a bank inhabited by quail-like creatures a little smaller than rabbits. Cheyara wrinkled her nose as Flora set a snare she had made from wire and a stick.

'We can synthesise protein—make food—that's suitable for your needs.'

'The food you give me is…not complete.'

She set the snare and they moved on. Later, Flora split

a rotten log with a knife, prizing out a giant grub. It was fat and pallid and writhed in her hand. The grub burst when she bit.

Flora seemed to know this forest as intimately as her home range. Over the last few days, Flora had acted with casual familiarity on the plateau, pointing out the routes to mountain passes that were invisible to Cheyara. Cheyara supposed that this, too, was a product of the memories that were inherited from past Matuas.

It was a day two and Biloko was close to the horizon. Cheyara was shocked about how far they'd travelled in a day. By the time they crested the ridge her legs, buttocks and the small of her back ached. Her shoulders were sore and she was very grateful to lay her pack on the ground.

Heron had some unsettling news.

'The weather satellite's reporting a storm front,' ey said.

'We're not going anywhere.' Cheyara said.

'No, but it's predicted to hit the entire region.' Heron looked at Flora. 'Including your House.'

Flora nodded, her face-spiracles pulsing. She was tasting the cold air.

'We have until yellow sun sets,' she said.

Cheyara looked at Heron, who shrugged.

Flora found a flat stone with a depression in it and ground the berries. She scooped the pulp into a plastic container provided by Cheyara. Then she dipped her hands in a stream that ran through the cirque. The stream was half-covered in ice and would surely be frozen in a matter of days.

Cheyara watched the clouds gathering over the mountains. A chill wind was blowing and the conditions were deteriorating with a frightening speed. This was typical of high-altitude environments.

'Why do the Matuas come up here?' She asked Flora. This was an outstanding question from the biologists. They did not understand, from an evolutionary point of view, why such a journey was undertaken. Surely it would be less risky to find a cave at the foot of the mountains, like the Chorelle and many other large animals? Nothing in evolution happened without a reason. There had to be some survival advantage to hibernating at altitude, but what?

'It is what we have always done.' Flora said.

Ten minutes later, snow was falling and they retired to the flier. Cheyara was grateful for the jet of warm air from the heater. Heron was soon forced to activate the wipers because large snowflakes were settling on the windscreen. Soon ferocious gusts of wind were buffeting a rocking flier. The light in the cabin came only from the information displays that Heron had left open. One smaller display showed routine systems status, outside temperature and wind speed and direction. The temperature had dropped to ten degrees below freezing and the wind was gusting at 115 kilometres per hour.

A larger display showed updates from the overhead weather satellite. They followed the progress of the storm from the mountains, into the valleys beyond. Eventually, the whirling spiral pattern of the storm moved over Flora's home valley.

'Welcome to Freeze,' Heron said.

The flier rocked again, the strongest gusts topping 130 kph. Cheyara had visions of the machine being overturned in a strong blast, which was not impossible.

For a while Flora dozed in the semi-darkness. Then her eyes began to flutter and she began to mutter words in her own language. Her head nodded, her chin resting on her chest. Then she raised her head and spoke directly to Cheyara, still in the humble language. Her eyes were half covered by nictitating membrane.

'I don't understand.' Cheyara said. Flora buzzed and clicked and eventually a few Earthian words came out. Her eyes fluttered.

'The House,' she said. 'The House is…broken.'

They tried accessing the drone feeds but the signal was gone.

'The House is broken.'

.

A few hours later when Biloko rose there was thick snow on the ground. It buried the flier's legs. Cheyara, stiff, massaged her limbs. Flora was squatting on the seat with her back to Cheyara. The humble's fingertips were pressed against the polycarbonate window as she surveyed a transformed land-scape. The cloud had mostly cleared and the snow-covered mountain peaks partly encircling the cirque were a stark white against the blue-purple air.

Biloko rose first, followed by Asali ninety minutes later. Neither shed much tangible heat. A glance at the display showed that average insolation at their latitude had fallen to about 1100 Watts per metre squared. This was still some way off the trough of deep winter, but there was no doubt Nyuki was falling down a climate rabbit-hole.

Heron was sucking a tube of food concentrate and fiddling with a display.

'We have a signal,' ey said.

The drone panned, revealing churned up mud, patches of snow and debris. Several grey huddles lay on the ground. An arm lolled from the nearest. The drone retreated, revealing the site of the house. The supporting umbrella trees were bare, grey columns. Between the tree-trunks was a large pile of rubble, consisting of broken walls, support struts and exposed wattle.

'Is the Matua…?'

'She is weak, but she lives.' Flora said, showing no interest in the livestream. She was gazing out of the window. Heron tried other drone feeds, but about half had been lost in the storm. Two were currently located inside the house.

'Inside?' Cheyara said. She could not believe that anything could live in the collapsed House. Heron activated the interior feeds. The first showed the remains of a store room. In infrared mode they saw a crushed barrel and smashed pot-shards. The other feed showed movement. Cheyara recognised part of the Juvenile Matua hatchery, with a caved-in roof.

The Matua moved slowly. She crawled in the narrow space between the collapsed roof and the floor. She sang to herself and fingered broken eggshells.

'She is singing to her children, who are gone.' Flora said, still not looking at the display. 'but she will not sing to me.'

The Matua looked straight into the drone's camera. She began to speak. Flora closed her eyes.

'She is talking to me, now. She says that I will die in the cold. She says that her children will live and that they will be new Matuas when the spring comes. She….'

The old Matua fell silent and turned from the drone, crawling slowly into shadow. Flora reached forward and swiped the feed closed.

'We should not watch her death,' she said.

Afterwards, Heron found another drone feed that showed several humbles making their way into the foothills above the home valley. Five new Matuas were making their way to a winter cave in order to hibernate through the winter. Statistically, Cheyara knew, one or two would make it through deep winter alive.

'I need to go and check my traps,' Flora said.

.

The trudge down the slope to the bank of the not-quail-rabbits was far more arduous than the day before. The snow had drifted in places. They found an animal in the snare, but the poor thing had frozen to death overnight. Flora removed the snare wire and deposited the carcass in her bag.

More than once Cheyara fell on her backside into a snowdrift and was helped up by Flora. She dragged Cheyara up and led her to another rotten tree-trunk. It was harder to crack than before. The grubs inside had begun to exude sticky threads for cocooning which dried as hard as iron. Flora picked the grubs out and threw them into her bag.

They were about halfway home when Flora paused, sniffing the air. She tugged at the sleeve of Cheyara's parka, indicating a need to hide behind a heap of shattered rocks. Cheyara followed her. Odd sounds were coming from an upwind direction. They hid and soon a pack of predators emerged from a snowy thicket. Breath clouded from the spiracles on their thorax and snouts. These predators were new to her, shorter and stockier than the vespon. They were a dirty, sandy grey colour. They had large teeth and bloody jaws. The blood might be good news. If the pack had recently fed, then they'd probably not want to pursue them. Cheyara thought of the gun that lay in her pack and prayed that it would not be necessary to break it out again.

The predators were following a trail down into the valley. One sniffed at the track Flora and Cheyara had made. Another glanced at the rocks. There seemed little doubt that the animal had their scent. Cheyara held her breath. Then she heard a bark and the pack began to move off. She sighed with relief.

On their return journey they startled several scavenger flitters who flapped away from a bloody patch in the snow. The predators had torn their prey to pieces, even devouring the bones.

12TH APRIL A.Y. 88

MISSION ELAPSED TIME: 597 DAYS.
LOCATION: NORTHERN SUBCONTINENT 2, NYUKI.
EMERGENCY PICKUP POINT AT ALTITUDE.

A day before the shuttle was due, Cheyara was collecting fresh water from the stream. The snow had made water collection more difficult. It was easy to slip, and Cheyara had to break ice with her axe to access the flowing water. Her hands were already numb so she kept dropping the canteens. Flora climbed out of the flier while she was stoppering the last canteen. The humble crunched through snow towards her.

'It is my time to go into the mountains,' Flora said. Cheyara nodded, unsurprised. The humble had grown thick down with a layer of fat underneath. The previous night she'd elected to sleep outside at the foot of the flier.

'I would like you to come with me.'

Cheyara put the canteen in her rucksack.

'I don't know that they'll let me….'

'They will. I spoke to them just now. The shuttle will wait while you come with me to the mountains. I told them I wanted you.'

'But why?' Normally the Matua completed the mountain pilgrimage alone.

'I know you feel…as if you have hurt us. Maybe that is true. But you also helped me. I would have died if you were not there. Your coming has changed things, for us. For me. For some…they will be more afraid. But not all of us. Not me.' She held out her four-fingered hand. Cheyara took it. It felt cold and clammy, and the end of the stinger brushed against her wrist.

'I will be glad to come with you.'

.

They were to set out the next morning. This was day seven in the cycle, with both stars rising together. Cheyara spent the afternoon packing her larger rucksack. One item was especially difficult to find. It had sat in the bottom of her luggage since they'd arrived on Nyuki. Until now, she'd not known why she'd packed it in the first place.

Towards evening the clouds descended and more snow fell. Cheyara and Heron waited out the snowfall in the flier's cabin, but Flora sat crosslegged outside. Soon, she was half buried in snow.

'*Has* this all been a horrible mistake?' Cheyara said.

Heron shrugged.

'Things are rarely black and white.' ey said, 'We made choices and mistakes. They made choices and mistakes.

Maybe no decision we make in the real world can ever be entirely right.'

'Taiyangren pragmatism.'

'I suppose so.'

The night was dark and for the first time in many months, Cheyara felt an inner peace. The cold high world of the mountains seemed utterly removed from the world's turmoil.

Unfortunately this reverie was truncated by a text message from Sonya. It read:

I'M GLAD YOU'RE OKAY. BUT THIS CHANGES NOTHING. YOU'RE NEVER GOING BACK.

'Does this never end!' she said.

'What?' Heron was lounging in eir couch, resting the back of eir head in eir interlaced hands.

She read eir the message.

Heron grunted.

'I thought things might be different. But they're just the same!' Cheyara said.

'No, they're different.'

'What do you mean?'

'We're not the only ones making choices.'

Cheyara thought of Flora pressing the activation button on the Flier. They were in new territory now. New, unexpected, difficult, exhilarating territory.

She hoped it would work out.

13TH APRIL A.Y. 88

MISSION ELAPSED TIME: 598 DAYS.
LOCATIONS: NORTHERN SUBCONTINENT 2. NYUKI.
EMERGENCY PICKUP POINT AT ALTITUDE TO THE
PLACE OF SLEEP.

Dawn came with both stars rising on cycle day one. Flora waited for her at the foot of the flier. The humble had a stone in her hand. Cheyara hefted her rucksack from the flier onto the snow. She climbed down the short ladder, sinking up to her knees in the white powder. She handed Flora a smaller rucksack with a supply of food and water. Flora opened the rucksack and placed the stone inside.

'I've got a lot of shovelling to do,' Heron said, eir breath puffing out in thick clouds. 'Are you sure you want to do this?'

'Yes,' Cheyara said, eyeing the mountains, which suddenly looked more threatening than picturesque. Light cloud was drifting past sheer rock faces. The weather satellite reported generally clement conditions for the day.

Before they left, Flora embraced Heron. Heron smiled, awkwardly.

'We could have done with some of that whiskey,' ey said, 'For a toast.'

'Are you going to be all right?' Cheyara said.

'Of course. You know, I should really be coming with you. Flora told me the route last night and it sounded treacherous.'

'You're still not strong enough. Besides, someone has to greet the shuttle when it arrives.'

'I know. Just be careful.'

Flora set off with Cheyara close behind. According to Flora, the Place of Sleep was two days away, via a narrow pass. They started by clambering over a sloped boulder field. Cheyara disturbed a mountain flitter with white down. The boulders were small but treacherous and more than once Cheyara almost slipped and twisted an ankle. There was a wide stream further up the valley that flowed below ice. Crossing was treacherous and Cheyara managed to soak a foot.

Above was more rough snow-covered ground. The trail was barely discernible but Flora seemed to know where she was going. It led around the bulk of the mountain. Flora, sure-footed, picked her way along the trail. Occasionally she would glance back at Cheyara and wait until she'd caught up. Cheyara, breathless and slow, recalled her own inept mountaineering on Leng. Still, at least on Nyuki she could breathe the air and walk properly. Earth-level gravity made all the difference.

The trail led slowly uphill and by mid-morning they were trekking between two mountains. On one side of them was a scree of boulders marking a steep arête, on the other a whaleback mound of drifted snow.

By the end of the morning, Cheyara was beginning to feel the altitude. They were already 3,000 metres or so above sea level, and her heart hammered hard against her ribs. Although she was already feeling breathless, she made efforts to maintain a brisk pace. Flora was now some way ahead.

Late morning they stopped for a food break. A cold wind was blowing down the pass and Cheyara had to pull on an extra layer. Flora sucked liquid sugar from a plastic nipple. The mist had descended and they could see maybe five hundred metres around them. The black boulders contrasted with white snow and sky. There was a light, almost invisible snowfall.

Despite Flora's presence, Cheyara felt utterly lonely. She wanted to speak but found that she had very little to say. She wasn't even sure why Flora had wanted her along on this expedition. She felt like a dead weight.

The previous events of the expedition already seemed like history. Something to watch on a video or read in a book. In this frozen landscape even the terrible last days of autumn did not pain her. Nor did possible censure back home or the Zungui threat. She felt numb, remote from the worries and cares of this and other worlds. She and Heron had done their best. That is all anyone can ever do. She smiled at the thought. Perhaps she'd also become a pragmatist.

'We must go,' Flora said, prompted by indefatigable biological need. Cheyara packed up her things and they left.

As the afternoon progressed they came to the end of a bowl-shaped valley and the rocks ahead were coated in ice. Cheyara activated the crampon function on her boots and made her slow and painful way up the slope, digging the points of the crampons in ice. If the slopes got more sheer she'd have to break out the ropes. Flora had hardly slowed at all.

Cheyara had reached to top of the rock face when the clouds began to break apart, revealing a shockingly dark purple-blue sky. The snow shone in the double sunlight and for the first time she was forced to don her shades. She reached the top with a thundering heart and gulping breaths. Flora, as usual, waited patiently.

Once she got her breath back, she looked up and the full majesty of the mountains hit her. The enormous granite buttresses with their conveyor-glaciers and snow-capped peaks shone yellow-pink in the bright afternoon sunlight. Cloud drifted over elevated valleys.

They travelled a little further, but Biloko and Asali were close to the western horizon. Cheyara began digging a shelter in a snow bank. Flora watched for a few minutes and then asked to borrow a shovel. She dug fast.

Night came. The air was still and the stars were bright. After dusk, Flora sat outside and lapsed into a trance. Cheyara retired to the snow shelter after giving her report to a drone.

·

In the red morning, Flora said:

'We must hurry. I must sleep soon.' Cheyara nodded assent, and she ate as they trekked. A pass led downhill in the face of a freezing wind. The chill blasts stripped the heat from her despite her thick trekking outfit. Flora didn't seem to notice. She hardly looked back anymore.

Cheyara was feeling stiff and exhausted in the cold, but somehow exhilarated. She hoped it wasn't just the altitude. But the human body has deeper wells of endurance and strength than is commonly realised. Despite her exhausted state, she did not feel the urge to stop or even slow down. Her heartbeat was elevated and she was always breathless. For the first time biometric warning lights were flashing in her visual field.

By early afternoon, she was forced to rest. Flora seemed restless but she consented, sucking sugar from her bottle. The weather was deteriorating. Clouds had rolled in and thick snowflakes fell.

'I'm ready.' Cheyara said.

The last ridge was the hardest. They had to cross a barrier of rocky, sharp stones. Cheyara baulked when she saw this, because it looked impassible. Flora took her hand and said:

'Step where I step.'

The trail up the slope was narrow and invisible from the bottom of the barrier. It took about fifteen minutes to summit and then they were looking down into a bowl-shaped elevated valley. Cheyara saw the dark holes of caves lined at one end. Each cave was marked by a snow-covered mound.

'Come,' Flora said and they descended. Cheyara glanced at the GPS location indicator. This place was over two thousand kilometres from the hibernation ground of Flora's Matua. She struggled to understand how Flora had known its location so precisely.

'An Old Matua came here a thousand winters ago,' Flora said, 'She found a cave and laid a stone at the entrance. This was before the Great Migration. For many winters, Matuas would come and lay stones at the entrance to the Place of Sleep.'

They had descended into the bowl and were approaching the largest of the cairns. Flora took the rucksack off her shoulder and produced the stone. She approached the mound, and placed the stone upon it. Cheyara rummaged in her rucksack, producing the small wooden chlorelle carving. Feeling a little foolish, She held it out.

'I thought….' She said, nodding at the cairn. Flora took it, breath steaming from her chest and face spiracles. Then she handed it back.

'No. Keep it. It is a spring gift.'

She led Cheyara around the base of the mound to the largest cave entrance. The entrance was a maw that was as dark as midnight.

Flora embraced Cheyara.

'Watch for me next spring,' Flora said. 'Because next warm-time, things will be different. I will build a new House in a new valley with many flowers and fruit. I will hatch many daughters. When summer ends I will be kind to my children because I hate unkindness. Matuas should be kind always.' She squeezed Cheyara's hand.

'You will be welcome in my House.' She nodded at the carving. 'Bring me your gift then.'

Flora handed Cheyara her rucksack and made her way along the uneven ground into the darkness of the cave, towards the long sleep, to dream of the kinder and better world that she would make after winter's end.

ACKNOWLEDGEMENTS

I'm lucky enough to be part of a community of very knowledgable and generous people who've been highly supportive of this project. First and foremost thanks must go to Liz Williams, my editor and foreword writer, for her invaluable suggestions and encouragement. Also to Dominic Harman, for such a terrific cover and to my beta-readers, Sue Thomason and Vaughan Stanger for useful comments on earlier drafts.

Indispensable world-building advice came from Stephen Baxter, Dave Clements, William Edmondson and Anders Sandberg. Stephen Baxter suggested that the Asali system should be binary and it's to Dave Clements that I owe the idea that the Abode Habitats should orbit the exo-Kuiper Belt planet Leng. Rory Newman, G.P., supplied essential medical details about venom, anaphylaxis, IVs and naso-gastric tubes. I owe the late biologist Jack Cohen a great deal for his ideas on credible alien design. Any mistakes, misinterpretations or distortions are my own.

Important sources included Sean Kinney's paper 'Stern Habitat: Colonization of the Kuiper Belt With Current Technology,' used as a reference for the design of Abodes 1 & 3. Stephen Baxter's article in *Spaceflight* 'Living space' (62:8, August 2020), about the BIS SPACE project pro-vided further useful technical details. The design of the 'Kalpana' space settlement was also consulted. Margulis, the Taiyangren settlement, is based in part upon the TU

Delft Starship Team (DSTART) design. DSTART is a project led by Angelo Vermeulen.

Stuart Armstrong and Anders Sandberg's 2013 Acta Astronautica paper 'Eternity in six hours: Intergalactic spreading of intelligent life and sharpening the Fermi paradox' (89:1–13) provided background detail for Zungui seed replicators, etc.

For the sociology of Abode Matthew Wilson's *Rules Without Rulers* on the possibilities and limits of anarchism proved useful. During the Msafiri confrontation Sonya quotes the Norwegian philosopher and founder of Deep Ecology Arne Naess.

The sharp-eyed might spot a cousin of Dougal Dixon's 'Vacuumorph' from his 1990 book *Man After Man* living amongst the Taiyangren. The idea of modifying humans to be able to thrive in space was explored by James Blish in his 1957 anthology *The Seedling Stars,* and dubbed 'Pantropy'. The concept has enjoyed a revival recently because it's becoming clear that space might be too alien an environment for unmodified terrestrial humans to settle. Sir Martin Rees discusses this issue and others in his 2018 book *On The Future.*

The story of Nasreddin and the singing horse has several variants and refers to a 13th century Seljuq satirist from Turkey. Wikipedia informs me that a 'Nasreddin story usually has a subtle humour and a pedagogic nature,' this one being a prime example. One version, 'Nasreddin and the Sultan's Horse,' is readable on the Sufism/Nasrudin page of Wikibooks.

I'm indebted to *Ice Ages: A Very Short Introduction* by Jamie Woodward for discussions of heat balance, glaciers etc. The basic idea for the humble life cycle came from the social insects episode of the 2005 BBC TV series *Life in the Undergrowth.* This dramatised the life of a bumblebee nest over a summer. My DPhil involved bumble bees, so in a way it felt like coming home. Like the Doctor, I'm rather fond of bumble bees. 'Humble-bee' is an older term for bumble bee.

Two useful sources on general ecology were Audley MacKenzie, Andy S. Ball & Sonia R.Virdee's *Ecology Instant Notes* and Chris Packham's 2012 TV series *Secrets of Our Living Planet.* Charles Cockell's textbook *Astrobiology* was indispensable. I also owe a debt to the ETUK Ecology online courses. Speculations on the nature of language are derived from Noam Chomsky.

The telepathic abilities of the humbles were inspired by the experiences of a number of anthropologists who have encountered apparently 'impossible' paranormal phenomena whilst living with indigenous people. A number of case studies are described in Paul Devereux's chapter of *Mind Before Matter,* edited by Trish Pfeiffer, John E. Mack and Paul Devereux.

Binary gender pronouns, already inadequate, are doubly so in Abode Year 86. However, there are as yet no commonly agreed post-binary pronouns beyond the singular they, despite the invention of over a hundred possible alternative gender pronoun systems. For this story, after some thought, I've opted for Elverson variant of Spivak pronouns: (ey, em, eir). See the Wikipedia page on Spivak pronouns for details. I found Joan Roughgarden's *Evolution's Rainbow* an invaluable guide to the highly complex topics of sex, gender and sexuality in humans and other animals.

CHRONOLOGY

COMMON ERA (C.E.)	ABODE YEAR	EVENT	LOCATION
2073		Corncrake Born.	Solar System
2081		Heron Born.	
2087		Magrena Born.	
2108		Earthian/ Taiyangren Exodus from Solar System.	
c.3100	0	Earth ships arrive in the Asali system. Start of the Abode calendar.	Asali System (c. 990 Light Years from Earth).
c.3161	61	Cheyara born.	
c.3178	78	Arrival of Expedition 1 on Nyuki.	
c.3179	79	October: Bobby Wong's death.	
c.3185	85	Discovery of Zungui in Samudra system.	
c.3186-3188	86-88	Expedition 2 on Nyuki.	

ALSO AVAILABLE....

WWW.MATTCOLBORN.COM

Printed in Great Britain
by Amazon